Sommer —

you'll be reading
Iowa history and
it will be fun!
(I hope!)

Mrs. MCCracken
11-04

D1711874

SUSAN MCCRACKEN

FOR THE GIFT OF A FRIEND

Friends United Press
101 Quaker Hill Drive
Richmond IN 47374-1980

This book is dedicated to my family whose encouragement has made the sequel possible.

Library of Congress Cataloging-in Publication Data

McCracken, Susan, 1950-
For the Gift of a Friend/ by Susan McCracken.
p.cm.
ISBN 0-94435035-6
1. Quakers--Iowa--History--19th century--Fiction. 2.
Teenage girls--Iowa--Fiction. 3. Family--Iowa--Fiction.
I. Title.
PS3563. C35248F59 1995
813'. 54--dc20   95-18285
                                                   CIP
                                                   AC

Table of Contents

SUSAN MCCRACKEN

FOR THE GIFT OF A FRIEND

1

Memories, Spring, 1853

Rebecca, would thee please milk Jezebel for me this morning?" Came Joshua's early morning request as I sat at the table, organizing my plans for the day and inhaling the fresh south breeze that came briskly through the open cabin door.

"Yes, Joshua," I called loudly, hoping my words would carry beyond the cattle shed where Joshua was obviously involved in some new project he didn't want to abandon.

Joshua Frazier. Who could have believed we would be married and living in our own cabin? Joshua, who had teased me so unmercifully on our long trip to Iowa from Indiana by covered wagon. Joshua, who had always been a thorn in the flesh to me; always there when I least wanted him. Joshua, who was now one of the most admired men in the Meeting, both for his ability to know what needed to be done, and for the way he respected and treated others.

My mind raced back over the familiar memories that so often presented me with a slow moving mental picture of people and events. The trip from Indiana had been such an adventure that even Joshua's teasing could not taint the memory. My family: riding in the wagon, walking through tall prairie grass, fording streams, sleeping under the stars, sharing our lives with the others in the wagon train. There had been times of sharing from the Word and prayer that had strengthened our earlier commitment to help the preparatory meetings in Iowa. Each of the families we had shared so much with, now received a silent prayer that their lives were being used by God in each of their new communities: Chestnut Hill, New Garden, and Salem.

"Rebecca, is thee coming?" came Joshua's second call, a bit of annoyance evident in his voice. Sighing, as I knew the memories would have to be put on hold, I quickly rose to take my light wrap from the now smooth peg near the door. Though the breeze felt refreshing in the stuffy cabin, I knew the air was a bit too brisk for no covering.

As I approached the shed, a slow grin spread across my face as once again thoughts of the past crept in. Jezebel. What a cow she had been! Though her years were well beyond those of the average cow, she continued to provide the two of us with an ample supply of milk. My mind raced back to the day Jezebel had gotten her rather unique name.

Father had acquired the spirited cow from the Hinshaws soon after our arrival in East Grove. Sweet Pea was her given name, but after she managed to break loose from her stake in South Woods that first fall, I felt compelled to rename her. I had allowed my youngest brother, Levi, to walk to the woods to bring her back for the night. When Levi did not return, I had begun a frantic search for him, having been left in charge of the younger children while our parents were in Salem. I was so angry at the cow, that once we found Levi safe and sound I renamed her after one of the most wicked women in the Bible: Jezebel!

I now gazed fondly at the cow's warm brown hide, and gently caressed her neck and flank. I suppose I should have quit calling her Jezebel when Father so graciously gave her to Joshua and me when we were first married. She certainly was not an evil cow! But old habits are hard to change, and I knew she would probably be Jezebel to me for as long as she lived.

"Where is thy mind?" came Joshua's inquiring voice from behind. "Thee has been staring at that cow for many minutes now and I believe she would like to be relieved of her burden of milk!"

Quickly grabbing the dented pail (more proof of Jezebel's not so perfect nature!), I began the gentle rhythm of milking. Thoughts of the present day's work to be done began to occupy my mind. The sourdough bread, Joshua's favorite, was already rising near the fireplace. I would have to rinse the cured ham I had been soaking for two days. It would still be quite salty to the taste, but when combined with beans or potatoes, it would be a wonderful addition to our often meatless diet. There was also washing to be done, since this was Second Day, though between the two of us there were not that many articles of clothing.

Joshua reappeared as the last streams of frothy milk filled the pail to nearly overflowing. "Rebecca, I believe I will ride over to thy parents' cabin to see if I might assist thy father with his fence building. There is no pressing work to be done here, and his leg has been bothering him the past few weeks. I'm certain he would be glad for the help. Fencing that new section of land he acquired from the Hinshaws will take a great deal of hard labor."

"He might *secretly* be glad for thy help, but don't expect him to welcome thee with open arms!" I said with a sad smile. Father was fiercely independent and still believed he alone carried the responsibilities for his family. His sternness had alternately scared me and angered me, but I knew beneath the tough exterior was the deep, abiding love of a man for his family. I would never forget the day he thanked me for plowing the field after his accident. Stepping in a deep hole while plowing had broken his leg, and nearly broken his spirit. His heartfelt thanks gave me a brief glimpse at the caring spirit beneath the gruff outer shell he often presented to his family. That, in turn, helped me accept the stern lectures he was known to provide his children!

"Will thee be home for the noon meal?" I remembered to ask as Joshua climbed on his waiting horse.

"No, I imagine thy mother will prepare enough for me, and Jacob or Levi will insist I stay and eat with them!"

Jacob was the older of my two brothers. He was very fond of Joshua and often spent time with the two of us when he was not needed at home. His sturdy six-foot frame forced him to bend slightly to get through our low cabin door when visiting. He was accustomed to hard work, and at the age of twenty, ready to be on his own. I knew he felt the need to help Father, since Father's leg often made it nearly impossible for him to do the heavy work necessary for raising a good crop. I also sensed Jacob's desire to find a good helpmate, one of the Friends faith who shared his dreams and goals. Unfortunately, there were no young women his age in East Grove Friends Meeting, and he did not have time to travel to other meetings in search of a wife! Knowing Jacob, not one given to sharing his inner feelings, he would be embarrassed to know I was even thinking such thoughts! I would have to make Jacob's future a matter of prayer, and leave the search up to God!

Levi, on the other hand, had always been bubbling with excitement over any small change in his life, always ready to share his feelings with others. I knew it was unfair of me to have a sibling favorite, but deep in my heart I loved Levi in a special way. Our experience with Jezebel had strengthened our bond of mutual respect, and Levi had often shared his heart's desires with me.

Pride swelled in my heart as I remembered the day Levi told me, before anyone else, that he felt called to be a teacher. He had asked me if I thought it would be an acceptable profession for a young man, and I reassured him our school needed his love of learning and compassion for those less gifted. Even though he was only fifteen, he was teaching twenty young children in the new school built the previous year. I would have to visit him before school let out for the session and give him my encouragement.

As I began to tackle the earlier planned tasks of the day, memories continued to seep into my thoughts. My sister Abigail was still at home, but planning to marry in August. She and her future mate would live near Springdale, seventy miles to the north of East Grove.

Joshua and I were fond of traveling to visit other Friends meetings within a few days' journey by wagon, and had visited the Springdale Friends Meeting at least once each year. On one such trip Abigail had joined us and was blessed to meet the fine young man she was now planning to marry. Daniel Todd was as fine a believer as I had ever met, and also very concerned for the plight of the Negro slave. Our first conversation remained etched in my mind for weeks.

The Springdale Meeting First Day School class had been studying equality of all men (and women, I might proudly add) when a friend asked if it was honorable for a Friend to assist a slave trying to escape to freedom when it was clearly against the law. Daniel had risen to speak, his strong, clear message having an effect on all present. "When the Light of God within the soul of man speaks of the equality of all men in the eyes of God, could there be any doubt that the Negro man, woman, or child deserves every freedom given the white man, woman, or child? Can there be any of you who believes that because one is born of dark skin they deserve the cruel bondage of slavery? My grandparents left their farm, home, and friends in North Carolina because they could not tolerate the attitude of that society toward the Negro race. I would hope we would all continue to uphold the Friends' teaching of equality of all God's children."

Not a soul had spoken when Daniel had finished, and when I glanced at Abigail's beautiful face, I was touched by her freely flowing tears. From that moment on, Abigail and Daniel were one in spirit, though their vows and lives together were to become future events.

I had always envied Abigail's beauty. She had the lightest hair, bluest eyes, and fairest skin of anyone I had ever known. There was also an inner beauty that had been spoken of by more than one admiring person.

Yes, Abigail and Daniel made a striking couple. I felt a twinge of envy, which I knew was not pleasing to God, but was difficult to suppress. Beautiful, sweet Abigail and handsome, fervent Daniel. A perfect match. I thought again about my marriage to Joshua. I had never been madly "in love" with him, as some would say, but I loved him in a different way. I loved his kindnesses to me and the others in the meeting; I loved the way Friends admired and looked up to him; and I loved the way he loved me. Totally. I knew Joshua would give his life for me if asked to do so.

I also believed God had chosen Joshua to be my helpmate.

After Joshua had been calling on me for a number of months and wished for us to be married, we spent several evenings praying together to be certain it was God's will for our lives. I had always believed I would know immediately when I met the man God intended for me to marry. Joshua and I, however, had spent most of our first years antagonizing one another! I couldn't help but chuckle when remembering the time Joshua asked me to share the noon meal with him after First Day Meeting, and I had said I would rather eat with a snake! Father had been listening, and I quickly assured him I would be happy to share my meal with Joshua but I had merely been explaining to him that I did not want to sit on the ground for fear of snakes! Poor Joshua! I had treated him badly at times. And yet I knew I owed my life to him.

The first winter I had been teaching the children in the community, Joshua had been working many long hours stacking wood for the winter months. When a sudden blizzard stranded three of us at the cabin, the wood pile provided warmth for our survival and a place for the horses to take refuge.

Yes, Joshua was good for me, no doubt about that, yet a small twinge of envy remained.

When the clothes were scrubbed and on the line, I set about the task of digging the last of the potatoes from the cache at the back of the cabin. The shovel pierced the soil and straw easily, but there were few potatoes to be found. Small and shriveled, I knew I would have to save enough to cut for seedlings as soon as the garden soil could be worked. Digging to the bottom of the pit, my find barely filled my now dirty apron. The ham would have to be made into soup with a few bits of potato and lots of water. Perhaps if allowed to simmer in the kettle over a low fire, it would become tasty in time.

Everything I knew about cooking I had learned from my mother. She had worked so hard to provide for the needs of her family, often with few supplies. Those first years in Iowa had been trying; meager crops and meager supplies, yet hard work and love between family members made the memories sweet rather than bitter. I knew Mother had wished for a better life for me, but here I was, struggling to cook a decent meal for my husband, working from sun-up to sun-down with very few rewards. Twenty-five years old, with nothing to show for my life except for two books in our "grand" library, and a husband who worked too hard for too little. Sitting down at the rough-hewn table near the fire, I slowly began to eat the warm slice of sourdough and sweet cream butter I had sliced for my noon meal. I sat long after the bread was gone, the weight of my failures becoming a burden too heavy to bear. Though the many memories that had colored my thoughts today were warm and pleasant, my present situation was less promising than I liked to admit, even to myself. Burying my head in my arms, I let the tears of despair I felt fall onto the wood in small puddles. Touching the thinness of my body, that other, deeper longing returned. I so desperately wanted a family, yet I couldn't even produce a child! What possible use could God have for me?

2

Friends Forever

The heaviness I had felt after my morning of memories continued throughout the week. I did not want to trouble Joshua, and I did not think he would understand my sorrow if I were to tell him. Joshua was concerned with the trials of everyone in the Meeting, and that was enough for one man to bear. I knew he sensed something was troubling me, though. When he asked if I felt ill one morning after breakfast, it was easier to avoid the subject than confess my feelings of inadequacy.

"Rebecca," he had begun, "Thee does not seem to be thyself these past few days. Is there something troubling thee?"

My reply was slow to come, but I wanted to make sure my words would not betray my true feelings. "I believe the spring season to be very beautiful, but it also means a great deal of work to be done. The soil needs to be tilled for the potatoes, and thee has farm work that must be attended to. In addition to the garden work, this cabin needs to be cleaned from one corner to the other. I'm sure when I can begin the garden work it will not be such a great burden."

It was not the absolute truth Friends believed one should always tell, but it was the most I could share for the moment. And I was concerned about the garden. The potatoes were our main food crop, and the prospect of a winter without our staple was bleak indeed.

"I sense there is more thee would like to say," Joshua probed gently. "I wish thee felt thee could confide in me."

"I do confide in thee, Joshua. I tell thee all the news as soon as I hear anything from our friends and neighbors."

"Thee knows that is not what I meant, Rebecca. There is something troubling thy soul, but if thee does not feel thee can share it with me now, thee knows I am always ready to listen."

Yes, always ready to listen. Joshua had always been the one friends and neighbors came to when any problem arose. I just could not allow myself to burden him with my feelings of failure as a wife and woman.

"Thank thee for thy concern, Joshua," I finally managed. "As I said before, I am certain I will feel more enthusiastic once I begin working in the garden."

"That's good to hear," came Joshua's reply, relief evident in his expression. "I believe I will check the fence line around our land this morning to make sure the rails are still in good condition. Would thee mind if I rode Samson?"

"No, I would not mind," I replied, a bit sadly. I had thought a good ride, perhaps a visit to one of the members of the meeting, might help me put my longings into perspective. But as Samson was the only horse I felt comfortable riding, I would have to be content in the cabin today, perhaps beginning the much needed spring cleaning.

"I should be back before the noon meal," Joshua called as he rose to leave. He was almost out the door when he turned and walked slowly to where I was sitting. Taking my hands, he gently pulled me to my feet, enfolding me in his arms. "I love thee, Rebecca Frazier, and I will love thee forever. Please do not doubt the depth of my love."

"Thank thee, Joshua," was all I could manage. As soon as Joshua left, I began surveying the cabin. I would work so hard there would be no time for dark thoughts. The corner bed came first into view. I would wash the heavy quilts today, take the ticking filled with goose feathers out to air, and clean the logs and floor beneath the bed while the bedding was hanging outside.

With renewed resolve, I began my tasks. Just as I finished hanging the clean quilts, I noticed dust on the dirt path leading to our homestead. What did Joshua forget now, I wondered. As the horse and rider came into view, I quickly realized it was not Joshua on the animal, but my dearest and best friend, Betty Johnson.

Betty and I had met soon after we arrived in East Grove, and had become soul mates, sharing our deepest thoughts. I had not seen Betty for several months as she and Luke, her husband, had been in Pleasant Plain helping Luke's parents on the farm. Luke's father had been ill for nearly a year and his mother had been trying to manage the homestead on her own. When the burden became too great for her, Luke and Betty felt led to move to the farm until help could be secured for his mother. Luke was a carpenter, one of the best in Iowa—or so I felt. His work was that of building furniture, wagons, and coffins, yet he lovingly crafted each piece, designed especially for its owner. I blushed a bit remembering how I had thought Luke would make a perfect husband for **me**. I had shared my thoughts with Betty only to discover later that **she** was the one who had captured Luke's heart! I hoped Betty had long since forgotten that part of our past.

"Rebecca!" Betty called, long before the horse was pulled to a stop. "Rebecca! Thee looks wonderful!" she exclaimed, climbing from her horse and nearly squeezing the breath from my lungs. Yes, this was my beloved friend. So warm and compassionate, so caring and giving. I wanted to savor the moment forever, knowing that my friend could not have arrived at a better moment.

"Betty, thee is a sight for sore eyes," I teased, gazing fondly at my friend. She had gained some weight, but her smile was as infectious as ever.

"Thee doesn't look too bad thyself!" she returned, squeezing my arm. "But thee could stand to add a little meat to these bones!"

"How are Luke and the children?" I remembered to ask.

"Luke is wonderful, as always," she said with a grin. "Jeremiah and James are doing well, also." Jeremiah was four years old and full of energy, while James was a quiet child, and my favorite. He was three and already knew how to read, thanks to his teacher mother. I knew Betty saved every spare dime she could to purchase books for her children. A rock seemed to form in the pit of my stomach as I knew that even if I had a child there would be no extra money for books.

"Tell me about Luke's parents and the meeting at Pleasant Plain," I finally managed.

"There is good news on both counts. Luke's father is feeling much better, but the doctor says his heart is damaged and he is not to do any farm work. Luke and I prayed diligently that we might know God's will for us in the matter. Luke did not want his father to have to sell the farm, but he really felt the need to return to his carpentry business. God really answered our prayers in a miraculous way.

"Luke's cousin, Philip, showed up on our doorstep one evening, having joined a wagon train with the idea of finding land for himself in Iowa. One of the families on the train knew Luke's parents were in Pleasant Plain and took him within a mile of their farm. Of course as soon as he mentioned the desire to purchase land, Luke's father worked out an agreement with him to farm their land and live with them until he found a mate, or wanted a cabin of his own. It was such a relief to all of us. I never cease to be amazed at God's goodness to His children!

"The meeting at Pleasant Plain continues to grow as well. Luke and I both enjoyed our times of fellowship with Friends there."

"Does this mean thy family is home to stay?" I couldn't help but ask.

"Yes, Rebecca, we're home for good!" she exclaimed with another quick hug. "Now, tell me about thyself...and thy wonderful husband."

I had to laugh at that comment. At one time I thought Betty and Joshua would make a good partnership, but Joshua was not interested in Betty. Of course I was too busy criticizing him to realize it was really **me** he wanted to court.

"Joshua is still doing what he does best: helping everyone in the neighborhood." Everyone except his wife, I thought with bitterness. No, that was not a fair judgment. I was the one who did not want to burden him.

"He always was the kindest man I ever knew. Remember how much he helped us when we started the school? Can you believe it's been almost ten years since we were teaching together?!"

"Those were some of the happiest days of my life," I said a bit wistfully. "I loved teaching, and I loved working with you. Then you had to go and get married and spoil it all!" I teased.

Betty and I had continued to teach for a year after she was married. When she knew she was expecting their first child, she chose to stay home and prepare for the birth. I had continued to teach for an additional year until marrying Joshua. There had been a succession of good teachers until Levi had taken over at the beginning of this school term. It was good for the children to have a male authority figure, and Levi was so patient with the children. He made a wonderful teacher.

As if reading my thoughts, Betty asked, "Is Levi still teaching at the new school?"

"There is one more week in the term, but he will return

next year. He really has found his calling."

"And just remember, Rebecca, thee was his first teacher, the one who instilled in him the love of learning!"

"He was such an eager learner, it was an easy job!"

"So tell me, Rebecca, how has thee been? What has been happening in thy life?"

I remained silent, torn between wanting to share my discouragement with Betty and wanting to keep it all inside.

Sensing my hesitation, Betty began to gently probe. "Rebecca, something is troubling thee, I can tell. Remember when I tried to protect thee when I was in love with Luke, and how we were both hurt by the secrecy? We agreed then to always be open with each other, no matter how great or small the problem. Please share thy burden; we can pray about it, if nothing else."

Sensing an opportunity that might never come again, I began to slowly tell my dear friend of my feelings of inadequacy.

"I can't even produce a child!" I finished with a break in my voice. "Thee has borne two beautiful sons for Luke and I have nothing for Joshua. I know he wants a family and I am sure I am a disappointment to him."

"Has Joshua **spoken** of his desire for a family?" Betty questioned gently. "Have you both prayed over the matter?"

"What is there to talk about? What man does not want a child to bear his name? A child to help with the care of the fields and animals? A child to train in the way of the Lord? One does not have to ask those questions, Betty, when one knows the answers!"

"I can see the pain this has caused thee, but I sense there is more. What else is the source of thy sorrow?"

"I am a failure as a woman, as well as a wife. My mother tried to warn me about the hardships of early marriage, yet I was so determined to find a husband and have a new life with him I chose to ignore her words. Grandma Burgess believed I was destined to do great things; that God had a special plan for my life. But look at me! Work from dawn to dusk as a common laborer, with not even a family to love and care for!"

With those words I turned away from Betty and began to walk slowly to the cabin. When she did not immediately follow, I assumed she had been so disappointed by my words that our visit was finished and she would soon return home.

I was surprised when her voice broke my thoughts. "Rebecca, I am sorry thee is so troubled. I am even sorrier that thee has not discussed this with thy husband!" Her words were kind, but I sensed a bit of annoyance as well.

"Joshua may not even want a child just yet! Perhaps he is wanting to acquire more land before beginning a family. A husband and wife must share these thoughts with each other if they wish to have a fulfilling life together."

"Joshua listens to the needs of people night and day, Betty," I said stiffly. "I will not become another problem he must try to solve. I am a strong woman, and I will work it out!" I finished, beginning to wish I had never started this conversation.

"Rebecca, thee can be the most stubborn woman I know!" Betty exclaimed, then added tenderly, "That is also what makes thee the **strong** woman that can handle the toughest situation she is placed in. Anyone who can plow a field all by herself is certainly no simpering female! But even though thee is determined to carry this burden, Rebecca, it is simply not fair to Joshua to keep thy feelings from him. It takes two parents for a child to be raised properly, and two parents should make the decision to bear children!"

"I will consider thy words, Betty," I finally said, hoping that would end our conversation.

Betty had more on her mind, however. "Now about God's call for thy life. Does thee not believe God chose thee to teach at the school?"

"Yes, I know that was God's will for me then. But that was a long time ago!"

"Has thee recently asked God about his special plans for thee?"

"How can God use a woman bound to a man by their marriage vows and bound to the four walls of a cabin?"

"Rebecca, I believe God has a different plan for thy present life, but thee must begin to seek that plan rather than allowing self-pity to shadow thy every thought!"

"Perhaps thee is right," I replied tiredly. "I will try to spend more time in the Word and in prayer."

"Good!" Betty spoke warmly, turning to leave. "Could we have a short time of prayer together?"

Taking my hands in hers, Betty prayed a simple prayer for God's leading in my life. Though I still felt the same deep sadness, the day was beginning to look brighter. And best of all, Betty and Luke and their children were back for good. Perhaps spending time with my friend would be just what my sagging spirit needed.

"There is one thing I need to tell thee," Betty said quietly. "I hate giving thee this news right now, but I wanted to be the one to tell thee before others in the meeting heard. Rebecca, Luke and I are expecting another child in October. I had hoped thee would guess my condition," she said, hands on her already thickening waist. "I'm so sorry if my good news causes thee to suffer even more," she finished sadly, knowing I would not hear her last words. I had already begun to run to the cabin where I could be alone to shed my tears.

3

Comfort in Times of Trial

The early spring rains which had prevented me from working in the garden finally gave way to sunny, drying days and the spring planting was completed in late May. Working with the soil and seed had been a catharsis for me, and I was diligently trying to be a good partner for my husband.

I had kept my promise to Betty to spend more time in the Word and in prayer. Each day as I completed a time of personal communion with the Lord, I felt a gentle peace settle around the uncertainties that seemed to plague me. I would simply have to wait to see what God had planned for my life.

The one thing I had not done, however, was speak to Joshua about my desire to have a family. I had spent many hours in the library at Salem reading every medical volume I could find. The human body had always held a fascination for me, and I loved devouring writings on the subject even though I could not always understand the technical terminology.

It was on one such trip that I found the information that kept me from discussing child-bearing with my husband. The section on reproduction stated very clearly that the inability to conceive a child could be due to a condition in either the male or female. What if Joshua were the cause of my barrenness? I would not have him feeling inadequate in this area when he made so many contributions to those around him. I would continue to ask God for a child and in the meantime simply trust Him to answer my prayer.

———————

It had been a good summer at East Grove Friends Meeting. Though the number of members remained steady, the spiritual growth of those gathering weekly was never more evident than in the Spirit-filled messages from various attenders each First Day.

One meeting in particular had been a great blessing to me. We women (the men, of course, gathering on the other side of the partition for their own meeting) had been sitting in the silence for perhaps an hour or so when Freda Hinshaw rose to deliver one of the finest messages I had ever heard in meeting. She spoke of George Fox, the founder of the Society of Friends, even quoting from his *Journal*. Fox had written,

> "And so our religion lay not in meats, nor drinks, nor clothes, nor a list of other negatives; our religion lies in that which brings us to visit the poor, and fatherless, and widows, and keeps from the spots of the world."

Freda had gone on to say that she fully supported the rejection of the traditional protestant sacraments of Baptism and the Lord's Supper because God was not distant, but present in the soul. If one wanted to commune with God, it could not be done outwardly, but must begin within the soul of a woman. Likewise, the Baptism that the Lord spoke of was a Baptism of the Spirit, the new Baptism his death would create.

I personally thought the idea of receiving a dunking in a river by an ordained male was elevating the position of one believer over another. Similarly, to me breaking bread with my family was the time for remembering together the death of God's son, Jesus. Being given a piece of stale bread and a sip of sour wine from some holy man was simply not true communion with God.

As I had sat in meeting that day, head bowed, looking at my plain gray dress, I understood Fox's words, though I personally preferred the thinking of his wife, Margaret Fell Fox. She had written,

> "Much can be missed by observing the outward things...for they can soon get into an outward garb and be all alike outwardly, but this will not make them true Christians...it's the Spirit that gives life. I would be loath to have a hand in these things..Away with these whimsical, narrow imaginations and let the Spirit of God which He hath given us, lead us and guide us."

Now there was a woman after my own heart! I understood the Friends desire to wear the plain clothing. I knew dye was expensive and added to the cost of cloth, thus taking away from the simple life. I also believed that God had used every brilliant color known to man when he created our world, and thinking of gray flowers, gray sunsets, and gray birds brought a smile to my lips. I would continue to abide with the Friends traditions, but I personally thought Fox should have listened to Margaret where clothing was concerned!

It was during our times of silent worship that I felt the Spirit of God within, and I knew without a doubt true communion must take place inwardly rather than as an outward sacrament. For that I was thankful to Fox for breaking away from the traditions of the Church of England.

I continued to see Betty at Meeting, but there was little time for personal visits. With two children under foot and the third growing larger each day, it was all Betty could do to keep up with her tasks at home. Luke was working from dawn to dusk to catch up on the work he had missed while staying at Pleasant Plain, so he had little time to spend with his family.

In early October when the harvesting of my garden was complete, I felt the urge to visit Betty. Perhaps I could watch the young boys for her so she could have some time for herself. I had not previously had the courage to spend time with her children, knowing the feelings of longing they would reawaken. I knew I was selfishly thinking only of myself, however, and finally made up my mind to ride over to the Johnsons.

Samson provided me with a delightful ride across the countryside. As I gazed at the myriad of colored leaves that were starting to fall, their beauty was breathtaking. Plain gray indeed! Nothing was more colorful than God's handiwork!

Arriving around the eighth hour, I was surprised to see there was no smoke coming from the chimney. Surely Betty had needed a fire to prepare the morning meal and take the chill out of the air. The boys, usually out running about, were nowhere to be seen. Sensing something amiss, I cautiously approached the cabin door.

"Betty? Is thee home? Luke? Jeremiah? James?" I called before knocking.

"Rebecca!" came a call from the carpentry barn. It was Luke, and the look on his haggard face was grim.

"I'm so glad to see thee!" he said in a rush, relief evident in his voice. "I am so worried about Betty. Please, come with me to see her and offer thy opinion."

Why would Luke want my opinion on his wife? Something was very wrong.

"What is it, Luke! What has happened to Betty?" I demanded, not even realizing I was squeezing his arm like a vice.

"I don't know, Rebecca. Thee knows the baby is due at the end of the month, and until last week Betty was having no problems. Then suddenly she began to feel weak. The doctor said her blood pressure was much too high and she would have to remain in bed until the birth. She doesn't want to eat and she just lies there without even talking! What am I going to do, Rebecca? What will I do if something happens to Betty? She's my entire life!" he finished in despair.

Feeling shaken myself, I knew I had to remain calm for both our sakes. "Luke," I said firmly, grasping both his arms and forcing him to look directly at me.

"Luke, many women have had problems with childbearing and managed just fine. I have read a number of books on the subject at the Salem Library, and almost every problem associated with birthing a child can be handled if one knows what to do. Betty needs thee to be strong and reassuring, confident of her ability to bring this child to life. Now, would thee please take me in to see her so I might give her my encouragement."

With those words Luke seemed to snap out of the despair he had shown moments earlier.

"I'm sorry, Rebecca. I did not express much faith in God or my wife just now. Betty is such a part of me that even the thought of living without her scares me so!"

"I understand," I replied, but in reality I did not completely. The kind of bond that Luke and Betty shared was not often found in a marriage. I knew they each felt such a part of the other that losing a partner would be like losing part of one's soul. In some ways, it was almost a relief to me not to feel so attached to Joshua. I would certainly grieve if anything were to happen to him, but it would not be the wrenching emotional nightmare that Luke or Betty would face.

Entering the dark cabin, I was immediately taken back to the illness of Betty's mother, nearly six years earlier. She had a lung disease that had gradually weakened her body until she had passed on to be with the Lord. Now it was Betty who was lying motionless in the bed.

Walking quietly to where she slept, I called her name.

"Rebecca..." she whispered, "I am so happy to see thee!" a smile playing about the corners of her mouth.

"Betty, what has happened? Can thee tell me what the doctor said?"

"When Dr. Jones was here from Salem a week ago, he told me he thought I had a mild case of toxemia of pregnancy. My blood pressure was too high, and my feet and hands were quite swollen. He said if I would remain in bed for the duration of the pregnancy, the baby and I should both be fine.

"Luke, of course, worries so much about us. He was so kind to take the boys to stay with Joshua's mother. She had volunteered to keep the boys anytime I might need her, and Luke felt I would be more inclined to rest if they were not underfoot."

A feeling of guilt came over me at her words and I felt a flush creeping into my cheeks. Here I was, a young woman with few responsibilities at home, yet I had never even offered to come and take the boys for a few hours, let alone a few weeks. Joshua's mother would enjoy the boys, I thought bitterly, since she had no grandchildren of her own. But I still should have been more considerate of Betty's condition. Why was I always the last one to be of help?

"What is troubling thee?" Betty asked quietly.

Wasn't that just like Betty? Lying ill in bed all day, yet still perceptive to my feelings. "I just wish I had volunteered to keep your sons," I replied. "I'm sorry I haven't been a better friend to thee these past few weeks. I suppose I've been so busy trying to finish up the fruit and vegetable harvest that I didn't think about thee needing help."

"Rebecca, I would not have asked thee to keep the boys if thee had offered! I would not do that to a friend who is desiring a family as much as thee. I know the boys would be a constant reminder of something thee so badly wants."

"Am I so transparent that thee can read my thoughts when I am several miles away?" I asked, a bit embarrassed.

"That's what friends are for, Rebecca, remember? To understand the needs of the other and then do the best they can to meet those needs."

"So tell me," I asked again, trying to get back to the subject of her condition, "what can I do to help thee until the baby is born?"

"Thee can give me information. I know thee has been spending a number of days in the Salem Library, and I have a feeling thee might have been reading about childbirth. Did thee happen to read anything about toxemia?"

I felt my face burning. Even though we were best friends, I was embarrassed to know Betty had figured out why I had been spending so much time in the library. Finally, I decided that what she wanted to know was more important than my feelings.

"Yes, Betty, I have read some about toxemia. I am not certain what the doctor has told thee, but from what I have read toxemia of pregnancy is a condition occurring anytime during the last half of pregnancy. The symptoms are an increase in blood pressure, sometimes accompanied by fluid retention and protein in the urine. When mild, it can be treated by bed rest and sedation. The doctor must believe thee has a mild case that will respond to bed rest. Did he give thee any sedative?"

"Can't thee tell?! I have nearly fallen asleep twice since thee came! All I feel like doing is sleeping!"

"Good!" I told her encouragingly. "Sleep is exactly what thee needs. How is the swelling?"

She pulled the heavy quilt from her feet and I could see they were still swollen, but not as badly as I feared. Gently pressing my thumb into the fluid around the ankle, I found the indentation to be visible, though it quickly disappeared. A good sign.

"Thy feet look good for thy condition. I think if thee will continue to rest, everything will return to normal when the baby arrives."

"That is so good to hear!" she exclaimed. "The doctor was in such a hurry when he was here. Whenever I attempted to ask him a question, he would answer with a grunt—or not at all. I am so glad thee has spent so much time reading these past two years!"

Now it was my turn to be puzzled. How had Betty known I had been spending time in the library for two years? I was not certain I wanted to know the answer!

"What else can I do for thee besides building a fire?" I questioned, preparing to leave so she might rest.

"The only other problem I have is Luke. Did thee notice the grim look on his face when thee arrived? No matter what I say to him, he remains fearful. It's not good for his health—physical or mental!"

"First of all, thee must know that one of the reasons Luke is so worried about thee is because thee does not want to eat. I will try to reassure him about thy condition if thee will promise to eat on a regular basis. He did seem to be in a little better frame of mind after we first spoke."

"I'm so grateful to thee for coming today, Rebecca. I will try to eat more in the future," Betty said faintly, as she drifted back to sleep.

After having built a warm fire, I quietly left the cabin, searching once again for Luke. I found him in the place where he spent most of his time, working on a cabinet in his shop. I explained to him everything I knew about toxemia and when I left he seemed much more at peace than he had earlier.

Telling Joshua about my visit later that evening, I couldn't help but notice the warmth and admiration in his voice.

"I didn't know thee knew so much about childbirth, Rebecca; where did thee get thy knowledge?"

Careful with my answer, I merely said, "The body has been a topic of interest to me for a number of years. Remember all those days when we went to Salem and I stayed at the library while thee did thy errands? I was reading medical books to pass the time."

"Thee is one remarkable woman, Rebecca Frazier, one remarkable woman!"

For the first time in months I felt I had really made a difference in someone else's life. Sleep was a peaceful finish to a rewarding day.

4

Passing Meeting

I continued to visit the Johnson homestead twice a week until the birth of their daughter, Ruth, on the first day of the eleventh month. Betty had been true to her word and had continued to rest and eat properly, thus minimizing the effects of the toxemia. The baby's birth, however, was traumatic; an event I would never forget.

I had been visiting Betty on the second and fifth days of each week, my main mission that of providing encouragement to both Luke and Betty. When the last day of the tenth month passed with still no news of the birth, I could not contain my curiosity. I decided to pay a call even though it was not my regular day to visit.

When I arrived I found it strange that Luke did not appear to be anywhere on the farm. The closer Samson and I came to the cabin, the louder came the moans from within. Instantly I knew Betty was in labor, and I supposed Luke to be by her side. I nearly turned the horse around to go back home, believing the birth of a child to be an event shared with family members only. Something kept me from leaving, however, and I now truly believe it was the Holy Spirit, persuading me to remain.

The cabin door was ajar as I approached hesitantly, and, looking in, I could see Betty on the bed. Luke, however, was nowhere in sight. Careful to knock, I was relieved to hear Betty call my name.

"Praise the Lord thee has come!" she said, her voice strained. "Luke has gone for the doctor, and I don't know if I can keep this child from entering the world before he returns," she said between contractions. "Please see if the water in the kettle over the fire is hot yet. Thee may need to set it directly on the coals if it is only lukewarm."

Once again, my readings on childbirth were put to use. I tried diligently to remember exactly what one should do when in this situation. I checked the kettle water and it was nearly boiling; a relief. Betty had already prepared clean pieces of white cloth and a small, soft blanket for the new arrival. I quickly washed my hands with a piece of lye soap and a bit of the hot water, nearly burning the skin. I knew the importance of killing any bacteria that might be under the nails or in crevices.

"Rebecca, something does not feel right," Betty called in anguish. "I hate to ask thee to do this, but could thee please look and tell me if the baby's head is emerging yet?" Just as she was finishing, another contraction sent her into loud moanings. I had never realized the pain a woman had to endure to bring life into being!

Knowing I must do everything in my power, I quickly lifted the covers to look for the head. I hoped the gasp I felt escape my lips was not heard by Betty. For what I saw was not the head at all, but what appeared to be the heel of one foot. A breech birth!

"What is it, Rebecca, please tell me!" Betty gasped as the pain receded a bit. "Say something! What is wrong?"

Trying not to panic, and praying frantically that Luke would soon return with the doctor, I tried to recall the instructions for breech birth. I seemed to remember reading something about the need to turn the baby, especially if it was the first child. But I also recalled that if the mother had successfully delivered other children, it proved the pelvic bones were large enough to accommodate the head, which was the main concern when the head did not emerge first.

I knew I was not knowledgeable enough to try and turn the baby. I also knew the risk of infection would be much greater if my hands were to enter the birth canal. Permanent damage was a possibility if the birth were allowed to proceed naturally, but it seemed the only choice I could make.

"This child wants to land on his or her feet, instead of coming headfirst," I tried to respond lightly. "I want thee to continue to push when the next contraction occurs, and let's see if we can not get this child into its new life!"

There was no response as Betty was already immersed in another wave of pain. The baby's legs had now fully emerged, and I knew the rest of the child must come with the next contraction to avoid damage. "Thee is doing so well, Betty," I said encouragingly. "One more strong push and I think she will be here!"

"It is a girl... thee can tell?" she asked, panting.

"Just concentrate on pushing with all thy strength. This may be the most important thing thee has done in thy life!"

I said a quiet prayer for the health and well-being of this precious child struggling to enter the world. As soon as the next contraction began, I could tell Betty was indeed doing her best to deliver the child. I was never so relieved in my life when the head squeezed through and I heard the first feeble cries of the child Betty and Luke would name Ruth Marie. She had already overcome one obstacle, just as her namesake had overcome many.

When Luke arrived with the doctor, Betty was lying in the bed with Ruth in her arms, a look of tenderness reserved for such special moments. The doctor examined both mother and child, and finished the details of the birth.

A surprised look appeared on his crusty face when Betty

told him of the breech position and my help with the labor and delivery. "It's a good thing you knew nothing about delivery," he said, turning to me. "However, young woman, I would hate to think what might have happened had you tried to turn the child. It's just fortunate that Betty has had other children and there was ample room for the baby's head. It's such a problem for women to have children when there is no doctor within a few minutes travel. It is easy for me to treat my patients in Salem, but you families out here on these farmsteads have to have a little luck involved for things like this to occur with no major problem."

"It was not luck, Doctor," Betty said firmly. "I believe the hand of God was here assisting with this birth. I also believe the extensive reading Rebecca has done on the subject of childbirth made her a valuable asset in the delivery of this child!"

For the first time, the doctor seemed to really see me standing there in the cabin. "And just where did you happen to do this reading?" he asked, a look of skepticism on his face.

"I have spent many hours reading medical logs and journals at the Salem Library the past two years," I said quietly, not wishing to argue with this man who obviously thought so little of my efforts.

"There's more to know about the delivery of babies than one can read from library books!" he said angrily.

Luke finally stood. "Betty and I are both grateful for thy services, Doctor, and I, for one, am glad Rebecca was here to assist Betty."

"Humph!" the doctor grunted, gathering his instruments and preparing to leave. "I'll leave you now," he said, turning back to Betty. I don't suppose you need instructions on child-rearing since this is your third." And with that he walked briskly out the door.

"He must have a lot on his mind," Luke said with more kindness than I felt the good doctor deserved.

"He was rude to Rebecca, Luke," Betty said, quickly coming to my defense. "I dread to think what might have happened if she had not come when she did."

"The important thing is that both thee and our precious Ruth Marie are in good condition," Luke said gratefully, pulling up a chair near the bed.

Sensing I was intruding in a family moment, I quickly said good-bye and headed for home.

The ride back was one of confusion as I tried to discern what else I could have done under the circumstances. My ears were still ringing from the doctor's admonition. I was not deliberately trying to usurp his position as a doctor; why had his words been so unkind? Maybe it was time I quit going to the library and concentrated on my activities at home and meeting. I then wondered how my life might have been different if I had been given the chance to increase my schooling. Would I have dared pursue a career in medicine when the only doctors I had ever known were men? Probably not, I thought regretfully.

Joshua was pacing the floor when I entered the cabin. It had been dark for some time now, and I knew he was anxious to know what had gone on at the Johnsons.

"It is a girl, Ruth Marie, and she is doing well," was all my weary mind could share.

"That is a relief! I was afraid something serious had happened after Betty's bout with toxemia. Was it a large baby?"

"I really could not say, Joshua. She seemed average to me," I said wearily, just wanting to fix a bite to eat and go to bed. How would I know if she were big or not? I had nothing with which to compare her.

"I fixed a pot of rabbit stew from the game I managed to find this afternoon. I used some of the potatoes and carrots from thy garden. I hope thee does not mind."

I smiled gently at my loving husband. I knew few men who would be willing to prepare a family's meal, commonly believed to be a woman's work.

"I am grateful. I do smell something quite enticing! I did not know I had married such a talented man!" I teased.

"Thee is the talented one, Rebecca. Cooking a rabbit and adding a few vegetables hardly requires great ability!"

After a bowl of delicious stew, we spent time together reading from the Word and praying. We asked for a special blessing on the lives of Luke, Betty and their children. Though I quickly retired to the corner bed, I found sleep hard to summon. As time passed, Joshua joined me and fell quickly asleep. His even breathing and occasional snores were comforting, but they could not ease the pain of rejection I had felt from the doctor. Why could I not be content with married life like the other women in the meeting?

The weeks that followed Ruth's birth were busy as we began preparing for Abigail and Daniel's wedding. Since they each came from different meetings, they had to pass approval at both Springdale and East Grove before setting a date. The committees of two men and two women from each meeting had reported to their respective monthly meetings after considering Abigail's and Daniel's suitability for marriage. Fortunately, they both felt the two young people would be an asset to the Springdale community, and that both were spiritually mature enough to handle the responsibilities of marriage. Daniel and Abigail both felt relieved to have passed both meetings and publicly declared their continued intentions of marriage. All this was recorded in the two monthly meetings and the wedding date was set for the first day of the third month.

Knowing the possibility of a blizzard in the third month, I wondered why they had not chosen a later spring date. I supposed they simply did not want to wait any longer to begin their life together.

The marriage would take place at East Grove, and a small wedding dinner would be held at our parents' cabin. Father and Jacob had been working fervently to add two additional rooms to the cabin. Mother had wanted the extra space for a number of years, and the prospect of having overnight wedding guests was just what she needed to get the men into action. The logs had been cut in the fall, but the work had gone slowly in the cold of winter. Hopefully, the finishing touches would be completed before Daniel's family arrived from Springdale a few days prior to the ceremony. Abigail had asked if Daniel's sister, Martha, might stay with Joshua and me as they would still be short of sleeping space. I had readily agreed, looking forward to a visit with someone from another part of the state.

The James family arrived two days before the ceremony to help with the preparations. The men were more than happy to help Father and Jacob with the extra fireplace they were constructing at the end of the new addition. The beds had already been built and covered with warm bedding, and the rooms would be cozy with a crackling fire. Jacob and Levi would inherit them when the wedding was over.

Thankfully, the day of the wedding was clear and the sun warm, taking the chilly edge off the cold air. Daniel had secured a civil marriage license before traveling to East Grove. I knew Father and some of the other older men in the meeting felt this was not a necessity; that being married in the presence of God and Friends was all the approval one needed to begin a life together. I was secretly pleased that Daniel had wanted to begin their marriage with the legal document. I sometimes wished Joshua had secured a license for us, but that was one belief he shared with Father.

The ceremony was in simple Friends' tradition, a solemn but joyous occasion. When everyone finished signing the certificate of marriage, Friends were invited to the meal at the cabin. It would not be a feast by anyone's standards, but the food would be wholesome and nutritious.

I had been enjoying Martha's visit in our home, and was pleased when she told me she was going to go to an academy to further her schooling. She had no desire to marry just yet, and actually said she had no desire to be confined to the four walls of a cabin tending to the needs of a husband and children! I so wanted to confide in her, to tell her of my struggles doing just that, but the newness of our relationship prevented me from doing anything more than congratulating her on the choice. I secretly envied her, though I knew my life was of my own choosing.

When Abigail, Daniel, and his family were ready to leave early the morning following the wedding, there were tears from all, but Mother was especially sorrowful to see her last daughter leave. I knew it was not only because she would miss Abigail's help in the cabin, but also because there was that bond between a mother and her daughter that would no longer be the same. I vowed to include regular visits to Mother in the future to help ease her pain of losing her youngest daughter.

"Please come and visit us," Abigail whispered as we hugged good-bye one last time.

"I will," I promised. "I will make sure Joshua and I find the time for a visit to thy new home. I will be anxious to see where thee will be living!"

After everyone had left I spent the rest of the day helping Mother clean the now empty cabin, trying to be of comfort to her.

Would I ever feel this way if my daughter were to be married? I would probably never have the chance to find out, I thought bitterly. And then another heavy thought occurred. What if Abigail were to conceive a child before I was able to have one of my own? Was there never an end to the pain one must endure when unable to have the thing most wanted?

5

A New Call

My life settled into a routine following the wedding of Abigail and Daniel. Interwoven with necessary work in the cabin were visits with Mother and Betty. It was no longer painful for me to spend time with the Johnson children; indeed I had felt a special bonding with Ruth and looked forward to playing with her on the heavy quilt Betty kept on the floor near the crib.

Ruth was always smiling and laughing, just the way I imagined babies to be. Betty, however, informed me otherwise one warm morning in July when I stopped for a short visit on my way home from Salem. I was laughing at Ruth's antics as she played with a raccoon tail that Luke had prepared for the children, and I made a comment about her bubbly personality.

"Thee should have been here when the boys were first born," she sighed wearily, thinking back to those long days and nights. "Jeremiah was so colicky that I had to carry him with me during the day to keep him from crying. Then Luke would take over in the evenings, sitting for hours in the rocking chair, singing and speaking softly to him so I could get some much needed rest. It still makes me exhausted just to think about it!

"James did not suffer quite as much with the stomach pains, but the evenings were his rough times and I would walk for hours with his stomach lying across my arms until sleep would finally rescue us both!

"So you can see why I feel so blessed with Ruth," she finished, picking up the small baby for a quick hug. She was rewarded with a grin from ear to ear and a hand full of yanked hair! As the mother and child became engrossed with one another, that look of longing must have crossed my face.

"Here, Rebecca," Betty said quickly, "see if you can entertain this child for a bit longer while I prepare some milk and muffins for the boys."

It wasn't long until first Jeremiah and then James came bursting through the cabin door, leaving a trail of water that rapidly dripped from their wet bodies.

"Where has thee been?" Betty said sternly, though I could see the corner of a smile she was trying hard to contain.

"Father took us to the creek to swim!" Jeremiah exclaimed excitedly. "And guess what we brought thee...a turtle!" he finished, unable to keep the secret. "Father said thee would fix it for the evening meal, but James and I want to keep him! Can we, Mother? Please?!!"

"Keep turtle, pwease keep turtle!" James chimed in.

"I will have to speak to thy Father about this!" Betty retorted. "How would thee keep a turtle here at the cabin? In order to live, a turtle needs water nearby. And what would thee feed it? Does thee know what turtles eat?"

The boys looked at each other, clearly trying to decide just how far to push their mother. Just then Luke came through the door, barefoot with trouser legs rolled nearly to the knee.

"Boys! I thought I asked thee to wait for me before running back to the cabin," Luke spoke with authority, but his tone of voice was laced with kindness. "And what is this turtle doing in our home?"

"We just wanted to show it to Mother," Jeremiah spoke for the two of them. "We would like to keep this poor creature from the dangers of the creek—if thee agrees."

With that, Luke burst into laughter. Soon Betty and I were also giggling at Jeremiah's adult-like response. Seeing Jeremiah's downcast face, however, soon brought an end to our gaiety.

"I am sorry, Jeremiah," Luke explained, "we were not laughing at thee. It was the idea of this turtle, who was born to live in a creek such as ours, being in need of thy rescue. I suppose if thee and James would dig a small hole out back by the sheep pen and fill it with water, perhaps the turtle would want to visit for a while. But don't be too disappointed if it does not care to be rescued by humans, even young boys!"

James and Jeremiah quickly grabbed their new pet and ran out the cabin to pursue hole digging. As adults, we all knew the turtle would be back at the creek before nightfall, but there was no danger in letting the boys have some fun with it before its inevitable escape to freedom.

Sitting at the table with Betty and me, Luke asked me a surprising question.

"Has Dr. Jones been to see thee yet?" he asked casually.

"I do not believe Dr. Jones will be calling on me for some time," I said with a bit of chagrin. "Unless it's an emergency."

"I would not be so certain, Rebecca. I am not at liberty to say more, but do not be surprised if he stops for a visit in the near future."

Not being one who likes surprises, I eagerly asked him for more information. "Please, Luke, tell me why Dr. Jones would be interested in seeing me—or is it Joshua he has business with?"

"As I said, Rebecca, I can not reveal any more. In fact, I should not have said as much as I did. I just assumed he had already been to see thee. I can tell thee, however, that he was more impressed with thy help in the delivery of our precious Ruth than he let on that day!"

"He was not impressed at all, if thee will recall!" I said with a trace of anger. "He implied that Betty would have been better off had I not even been there!"

"As I said, I think he really was impressed with your knowledge of breech birth, and also toxemia."

"How could he be impressed?" I continued to question. "He hardly spoke to me, and the words he did say were not flattering!"

"Thee can thank me for enlightening him," Betty spoke up. "Remember when Ruth had that terrible cough last month and we finally took her to see Dr. Jones? I thought it was time someone set him straight on the matter of Ruth's birth. I made sure he knew thee was the one who came to visit when I was confined to the bed with toxemia, and thee was the one who explained the condition to me and helped me cope with the situation. I also made sure he knew it was thee who explained the breech position to me, and continued to assist with the delivery. I had no idea how he would respond to my words, but I knew thee deserved more respect than the good doctor afforded thee," she stated firmly.

"I am not sure what to say," I finally managed. "I suppose I should thank thee, Betty, but I thought perhaps the doctor was correct in his admonition. After all, I certainly have had no training in childbirth!"

"Nevertheless, thee did a wonderful job, and Ruth owes her cheerful existence to God and to thee, Rebecca."

"Thy words are kind, and as much as I would like to stay and hear more, I had best be riding home before Joshua wonders what has happened to me!" I finished, rising to leave.

"Once again, I thank thee for coming," Betty said as we walked out to the horse and wagon. "Thee doesn't know how much it brightens my day to have thee visit. As much as I love my children, I also love adult conversation with my good friend. Please come again soon!"

"I will, Betty. I really do enjoy thy family, especially Ruth. Although I love the boys, too," I added quickly.

"I know thee does. Has thee been to the library lately?" she asked eagerly.

"As a matter of fact, after I picked up the wheel Joshua had left for repair at the blacksmith's, I managed to spend an hour or so checking on the new arrivals. There was a new medical volume that someone had brought from Ohio and donated to the collection. I can't wait to return to read more of it!" I told her excitedly.

A look of wistfulness crossed Betty's face as she thought of the opportunities I had that she was missing. "I wish I had time to spend with thee, reading any book I chose!"

"The children will be old enough to take to Salem before thee knows it, Betty. Then perhaps we can go together and I can help thee watch the children," I said encouragingly, climbing into the wagon.

"That would be wonderful, but I fear it will be a day or two," she said with a smile.

"Until we meet again," I called as I guided the horses down the lane and onto the path toward home.

Later that evening I shared with Joshua the conversation I had with Betty and Luke regarding Dr. Jones. He seemed to be as puzzled as I.

"I suppose he wants to pay thee a visit to apologize for the way he spoke to thee the day thee helped Ruth come into the world," was Joshua's thought.

"I would be very surprised if that were to happen, Joshua. Thee did not hear the contempt in his voice when he learned I had helped with the birth!"

"It has always bothered me that he treated thee in such a manner, Rebecca. Perhaps time has helped soften his opinion of thee. There is also the fact that Betty spoke so highly of thee on her visit with Ruth. He is simply human, Rebecca, and humans make mistakes and later apologize for them."

"I suppose thee might be right," I said doubtfully.

As the days passed into weeks and weeks into months, thoughts of Dr. Jones and his possible visit grew more and more remote. Once again the fall harvesting had to be completed and I was extremely busy preparing the cabin for the winter. With no children to chink the walls, that unpleasant task was one I left until last.

As I was making yet another trip from the slippery river bank to the cabin with mud for chinking, I noticed the horses in the corral seemed a bit agitated. Shortly thereafter I knew the reason, as what should appear on the path to our cabin but Dr. Jones in his black buggy. He had one of the nicest rigs I had seen since settling in Iowa. His business must be quite profitable, I thought, feeling a bit envious again. Shaking those thoughts from my mind, I became excited at the thought of finally knowing the secret of this mysterious visit.

Knowing Dr. Jones to always be in a hurry, I quickly washed my hands in the bucket of clean water I had carried in one hand from the river, knowing it meant yet another trip for drinking water before darkness set in. There was no time to change my now mud-splattered dress; I supposed it was time for Dr. Jones to know the real me: childless settler's wife doing menial tasks. I felt the warmth rise in my cheeks as I thought of my disheveled appearance.

"Mrs. Frazier." Dr. Jones spoke in his usual clipped manner, not bothering to climb down from the rig.

"Dr. Jones," I replied, determined not to act like a loose-tongued simpleton!

"I happened to be at the Emry farm south of Pleasant Plain today, so it was convenient for me to pass this way on my return trip to Salem. There is a matter I have been meaning to speak with you about for some time now, but my days seem to be filled with countless emergencies, not the least of which are the births of numerous children. It is my opinion that every woman in this part of the territory decided to start or add to their family once they were settled!"

How was I to reply to that statement?! Everyone but me, I could have said, or had thee not noticed? No, it probably never entered his mind that he had never been to this particular homestead to deliver any new family member! I remained silent, however, waiting for him to finish his monologue.

"Mrs. Johnson was none too pleased with my lack of bedside manner the day she delivered the new child...girl, was it? Yes, she let me know in no uncertain terms that you had indeed been helpful to her when she was ill with that blasted toxemia. She also assured me that you were well read on the subject of breech birth and that you instructed her well."

Then Dr. Jones did something I had never seen before: he actually chuckled! Not a roaring laugh, mind you, but a chuckle, none the less.

"Must admit I admire her spunk! Now, to get right to the matter at hand.

"As I said at the Johnsons, Mrs. Frazier, one can not know much about the birthing of babies from reading in a textbook. I did not mean to be cruel, but it is simply a fact."

Why was it that even now I was embarrassed by his comment? Maybe cruelty had not been his intention, but his words had certainly hurt, nonetheless.

"As I told you that day, there is simply too much territory for one doctor to handle. The birth of a child is one of the most common tasks I am called to assist with, and often there is no reason for medical expertise at such occurrences. Likewise, minor injuries, broken bones, lacerations, contusions and so forth could well be treated by a lay person who had been trained to do so."

Where was he going with this conversation? It was amazing to hear Dr. Jones say so much at one time, especially considering all my past encounters with him had been one-sentence dialogues!

"If you are interested in the job, I could teach you enough to get you by, especially if you would continue with your readings. I might even loan you a few of my text books if you would make certain they were returned to me in satisfactory condition."

Wait a minute...WHAT job?! What was he speaking of?

"Well, if you need time to think it over, I suppose I could give you a few days to do so.

"Mrs. Frazier!"

The sternness of his voice woke me from my jumble of thoughts. Was Dr. Jones speaking to me, Rebecca Frazier? Was it possible that he actually thought I might be of assistance to him in his practice? I had not been allowed to attend school past the age of fourteen. How could I possibly be of any use to this highly educated man?

"I assume your silence means you will consider my proposition. I will expect to hear from you within the next two weeks. Good day, Mrs. Frazier."

Finally finding my tongue, I managed to call out a muffled thank you, though I doubt the sound could be heard over the creak of the buggy and the pounding of the horses' hooves on the hard dirt surface.

Imagine that! Dr. Jones actually thought I, Rebecca Frazier, could assist him in his practice. What had made him change his mind about me? I imagined the words of Betty had been a powerful force in this change of heart.

What would Joshua think of this new development? Would he resent a wife who did something besides tend the fireside? And Betty? Would she be in favor of such a venture? She had certainly come to my defense where Dr. Jones was concerned, but would she really be in favor of a woman doing such a thing? And my family? Father, especially, had a firm idea of the role of each marriage partner. Would he believe it was not the place of a woman to be so employed?

One thing was certain: this would have to be a decision made on my knees in prayer, with my husband. Even the meeting, perhaps, could cast light on the subject. If this was indeed God's calling for my life, I did not want to miss the opportunity!

6

The Quest For Happiness

The decision I had to make would not leave me. It followed me as I worked in the cabin, it followed me when I went to meeting, and worst of all, it followed me to bed at night, blocking the much-needed sleep I so badly sought.

In the end, I knew the decision had to be mine. But was it wise to ignore the words of those who knew me best? Betty, of course, was my biggest supporter. Though our visits were not as frequent as I would have liked, each time we spoke she encouraged me to follow the Light within. My problem was knowing what the Light was revealing to me!

Father and Mother were surprisingly silent on the subject. I had supposed Father would be adamantly opposed to a woman (his own daughter, no less!) working beyond the homestead. When I asked him for his opinion, however, he simply said it was not a decision he could make for me. Mother, likewise, said very little, although the light that shone in her eyes when I explained the opportunity let me know she was in favor if I chose to pursue Dr. Jones's offer.

I had asked the women of East Grove Meeting to pray

for me, although I did not feel comfortable sharing the exact nature of my request. I knew each would be faithful in prayer, and I had to believe God would reveal His will to me if I were patient.

When the two weeks Dr. Jones had given me to make my decision were nearly complete, I still struggled with my response. Although I badly wanted to do exactly as he had proposed, I simply did not feel qualified. Nor did I feel comfortable leaving Joshua with added responsibilities on the farm. I had no idea how much time my chores would demand, which added to my dilemma. I knew Joshua would support my decision because he loved me and wanted me to be happy. In the end, it was Levi who helped me choose which path to follow.

When the day before my deadline dawned crisp and bright, I decided a ride through the wind on the back of Samson might clear my muddled mind. It was so occupied as I rode that when Samson pulled to a stop in front of the school house, I had no idea how we had gotten there! The children were just being dismissed as we arrived, so I thought a visit with my "little" brother might be just the thing I needed to get my thoughts on something besides myself.

"Greetings, Rebecca!" Levi called as he walked out with the last pupil. "What brings thee back to school? Don't tell me thee has forgotten how to read and write!" he teased.

"In all honesty," I replied, "I do not know why I am here! All I can tell thee is that Samson brought me and I thought a visit with thee might be nice."

"I do not know what is occupying thy mind, but this doesn't sound at all like the Rebecca I know! Come inside where the fire is still hot enough to warm thee a bit."

As I entered the room I was instantly transported back to the years I spent teaching children. The new school was quite different from the abandoned cabin where Betty and I had first begun our work. We had nothing but puncheon benches, a few books and slates and the love of learning we wished to instill in the children.

Levi's school, on the other hand, had wide, sloping shelves fastened to the walls beneath the windows for desks. There were storage spaces under the desks for books, and specially made seats for the students. I stood in awe at the size of the glass windows. Our windows had consisted of heavy waxed paper over the openings in the logs. How much brighter the windows made the school! No child should have an excuse for not learning in this setting! When I saw the new black stove in the front of the school, I knew education was definitely changing for the better.

"Thee must feel fortunate to teach in such a fine building," I couldn't help but comment, continuing to marvel at the improvements in the school.

"Yes, the building is wonderful, and I am thankful the Society of Friends believes so highly in the education of their children. I believe, however, that I could teach anywhere there were children who wanted to learn," he finished quietly.

"No wonder the children love thee so! Betty tells me Jeremiah loves to come to school, and he also loves the way thee makes learning enjoyable for them."

A smile lit up Levi's face as he thought of Jeremiah. "Now there is an ambitious child. Does thee know he could already read when he came to school? Not to mention knowing his multiplication facts up to five. Betty has not quit teaching, she has merely moved from the school house to the kitchen table!" he finished admiringly.

"So tell me, big sister, what has been happening in thy life these past months? It seems like a century since we have had a chance to visit."

Knowing Levi would give careful consideration to my predicament, I shared with him the visit from Dr. Jones and his proposition to me. I also told him the difficulty I was having in making a decision.

"I want to be obedient to the Light within, but I have

not been able to discern what the Spirit of God is saying!"
The anguish in my voice must have helped Levi understand
my turmoil. After some thought he gave me the answer I
needed.

"Rebecca, does thee remember all the sayings thee used
to recite to me? The ones thee said were Grandma Burgess's
famous words? There was one about the quest of happiness. I do not remember the exact words, but thee used to
quote it to me all the time when I was a young child.
Everytime we went to the General Store, in fact! Whenever I began begging Father to buy me something, thee
would recite it. Remember?" he asked, grinning at the
memory.

"How could I forget? I thought I was thy teacher both
at school and at home!

"Yes, back in Indiana one of my favorite pastimes was
walking to Grandma Burgess's house with you and Abigail
and Jacob for cookies and milk. Grandma used to whisper
her quotations to me whenever we were alone, and I believed she loved me most of all! Of course, now I realize I
was the only child old enough to understand and remember the words!

> "The quote thee is referring to says, 'The quest of
> happiness, per se, is mistaken and futile, and it
> can only come as a by-product of a life losing
> itself for others."

"And thee has provided a window for me to see the
Light within, Levi. Now I know what my answer to Dr.
Jones shall be!"

"I will be the first to call on thee when I have a medical
problem, Rebecca!" Levi said with a knowing smile.

My sweet Levi! How I missed spending time with him!

"Please come for a visit soon, Levi. Joshua and I would
both like to see thee more often!"

"Thee will be too busy for a poor school teacher to

trouble!" Levi said teasingly, though I sensed a hint of sadness in his voice.

"Nonsense! I do not expect to be very busy with this position, Levi. What woman of the community would want to entrust the birth of her child to an untrained woman?! Or what father would trust me to stitch a wound or set a bone for his child?! No, even though I will say yes to the opportunity being offered me by Dr. Jones, I do not expect my life to be much different than it is now!"

"We shall see. In the meantime, I will try to ride over to visit thee before the snow piles too high! I thank thee again for stopping by—even though thee really should not be riding around the countryside with no idea where thee is heading!" he finished with a laugh.

I gave him a big hug on my way out the door, surprised at the size of this growing young man whom I loved so dearly.

"Until we meet again!" I called, turning Samson toward home.

When I spoke of my decision to Joshua that evening, his reaction was exactly as I had predicted.

"I think thee will be a wonderful assistant to Dr. Jones," he said smiling warmly. "Of course I will miss having thee here all the time, but as I seem to always be involved in the quandaries of others, I doubt I will have much time to sit and pine for thy presence, snake lover!" he teased.

"I am not certain why thee kept pursuing me after my many rejections of thy attention!"

"Thee knows why: I knew thee was the woman for me a long time ago, and I was very persistent!"

"That thee was, dear Joshua! I do have one request of thee, however. Would thee have time to go with me to deliver my answer to Dr. Jones? Perhaps thee will think of a question that needs to be answered that I might neglect to ask. I seem to get tongue-tied when I am in the presence of Dr. Jones!"

"I would be happy to accompany thee," Joshua replied, pleasure coloring his voice. "When did thee think thee would make the trip?"

"Tomorrow," I said with a quick grin.

"I think I can arrange to go with thee, Dr. Frazier!"

"Please, Joshua, don't ever call me that! If thee had any idea how frightened I am of the responsibilities I may be assuming, thee would not tease me about this. What if I cause someone's death? What if a baby is born with permanent damage because of something I have done? How would I be able to live with myself?!"

"Rebecca," Joshua said quietly, taking me in his arms. "There is one thing thee must always remember. We worship a God who is in control of every situation when we believe in Him and are one of His children. I know thee will use this opportunity to serve the Lord, not for thine own glory. When God is in control, we cannot doubt the outcome."

"I understand thy words, Joshua," I said, still remaining a bit doubtful. "But I will still feel it is my fault if something disastrous happens!"

"Rebecca, thee must turn thy worries and doubts over to God right now, even before thee talks to Dr. Jones. God can handle any situation if we put our trust in Him."

Even though my decision had been made, sleep was still unreachable that night. The thought of mistakes and causing misery in the lives of others continued to haunt me. Finally, toward morning, I drifted into a dream-filled sleep.

When we were seated in Dr. Jones's office in Salem the next day, he was his usual man of few words.

"Has thee made a decision, Mrs. Frazier?"

"Yes, I have."

"Well, out with it! I don't have all day! Will you assist me with some of the workload in your area or not?"

"I will try," was all I could manage.

"Nonsense! You will not TRY, my dear, you will simply do as I tell you! When can you begin? Today?"

"Oh...no...I mean...I had not planned..." I continued to stutter, never dreaming he would be expecting me to begin training this very day!

"Very well, then when?" he asked sharply.

"There are a few questions we would like answered before Rebecca begins this apprenticeship—that is what thee would call it, doctor, is it not?" Joshua answered for me.

"Yes, I suppose one could say this is a type of apprenticeship, although it will not be a lengthy one. There are simply too many needs to be met and I do not have a great deal of time to spend on this project. Rebecca seems to have read a number of volumes at the library—at least that is what her friend Betty tells me. So it should merely be a matter of applying what she has read. Now—what other questions did you have?"

"How does thee propose to do this teaching? Will Rebecca stay here in Salem and work with thee?" Joshua asked patiently.

"I have secured a room at the hotel where she will stay for the course of the training. The amount of time needed will depend on how quickly she progresses, of course."

Dr. Jones must have been fairly certain of his powers of persuasion to have secured a room before hearing my answer! I felt a bit of anger rising as I thought of his presumptuousness! If I had not wanted the opportunity to serve, I would have been tempted to decline his offer after all just to show him!

"What about a salary? How will thee pay Rebecca for her services once the training is finished?"

"Rebecca will need to collect her fee for the services rendered at the time she provides them. I do not have time to chase about the countryside collecting whatever payment the various families can afford!" he said rather disgustedly. "If you think this is a way to earn a great wage, you had best think again. Many of my clients are homesteaders like yourselves who often pay with produce or donated labor."

Once again I could feel the anger surface. I had not even considered payment. I was offering myself as a service to others, not as a paid professional. Finally, I could remain silent no longer.

"Dr. Jones!" I spoke firmly, trying to keep the tremor from my voice. "Thee has never seemed to have any respect for me—not in the past, and not now. Even though thee has little regard for me as a person, I would like for thee to know that I spent many hours in anguish over this decision and never once did I consider whether or not I might be paid! I want to be of service to others, but now I am not even certain thee and I can work together. If thee has any doubts about my motives, or my abilities, please speak now so I will know whether I have made a mistake in choosing to accept thy offer!"

"Well, well! She does have a little backbone!" he said begrudgingly, a hint of admiration finally evident in his voice. "I was not criticizing your motives, Mrs. Frazier, I was merely answering your husband's question!"

"Very well," I said, looking him straight in the eye. "I can begin in one week, if that is satisfactory for thee."

"One week it is, Rebecca. That is your first name, is it not?"

"Yes, Rebecca is correct."

"Good. You may call me Charles since we will be working together each day. No need for formalities. Now, if you have no other questions I must check on a child with a high fever. I will expect you at eight in the morning one week from today. Plan to remain at the hotel for a minimum of one month. Then we shall assess your progress."

"Thank you for the...opportunity," I finished to myself, as Dr. Jones was already out the door and gathering the reins of his horse.

"Well, Rebecca, it looks as though thee has a big challenge ahead!" Joshua said as we rose to leave.

"I know so little, and I feel so inadequate!"

"Oh, I was not thinking of that challenge! I think thy biggest challenge will be abiding peaceably with Dr. Jones! He seems to hit a sore spot with thee without even trying!"

"Thee need not worry, Joshua," I said with determination. "I will show him that he has just made the wisest decision of his career!"

"That is the Rebecca I know and love!" Joshua said with a squeeze of my hand. "By the way...how do you suppose Dr. Jones feels about snakes?!"

7

Healing Old Wounds

My month with Dr. Jones was full of surprises and challenges. The days were spent following him from one problem to another, sometimes at his office, sometimes in patients' homes. After the first week, I gained a new appreciation for the demands on a doctor's time. And perhaps, I finally admitted, that was part of the reason for his lack of patience with those he encountered.

Riding across the countryside in Dr. Jones's rig gave me a chance to ask him some of the numerous questions I had after my months of reading medical books at the library. He was pleasant to me on those occasions, and I sensed he enjoyed explaining the intricacies of practicing medicine to me.

On one such day I finally summoned the courage to ask him about his family. When Dr. Jones did not respond for what seemed like an eternity, I was afraid he was reverting to the man I knew before beginning my work with him. Finally, after anxious moments on my part, he began to speak, his voice subdued.

"I was educated in Chicago where I met Julia, the woman who would eventually become my wife. Her mind was as sharp as a tack and I loved to debate the issues of modern times with her. She was also a beautiful woman and respected by those who knew her. Her greatest desire was to be a full partner with me in a medical practice in the city, though her parents were adamantly opposed. They believed, like many in their day, that the responsibilities of medicine were far too great for a woman to handle. They also believed a woman's first priority was producing and raising offspring for her husband." He paused, as if being transported to another time and place.

"Did she pursue her dream?" I couldn't help but ask.

"Yes," he said with great admiration, "in spite of her parents' objection she enrolled at the Chicago School of Medicine the year following my entry. We would often study together and she was so eager to do as well, if not better than I. Your inquisitiveness, Rebecca," he said, turning to look at me, "reminds me a lot of her.

"When I graduated and began looking for a place to begin my practice, I could not decide whether to remain in the city or pursue territorial medicine. I knew the needs were great in both areas. I had seen the sick and dying children lying in the city slums and felt a great compassion for them. But there was also the call of the frontier. I knew territory doctors were needed by new settlers, and I yearned for the esteem I knew would be mine as the only available doctor in the community. Even now rural doctors are often the only link between life and death."

"What about Julia?" I could not help but interrupt. "What did she want thee to do?"

"Julia wanted me to do whatever I wanted to do. She said she had no preference, though inwardly I felt she would rather I remain in Chicago.

"Eventually my love for her made the decision easy. I would stay in the city where I could continue to see her as often as possible, with the hope that she would marry me when she finished school."

"And were thee married then?" I inquired, not remembering him mentioning a wife or family in any of our previous visits.

"Yes, we were married the year following her graduation. We were able to begin a practice together and it was one of the proudest days of my life when I hung the sign on our two room office/living quarters that read JONES AND JONES, Doctors of Medicine!"

"Then what happened?" I asked eagerly.

"Our practice was slow at first, but eventually word got round in the poorer sections of town that there was a man and wife that would come into their rat-infested neighborhoods to treat the sick. And even better, the wife often asked for no more pay than a loaf of bread or the apple pie cooling outside the window!" he chuckled with the remembrance. "I never could convince Julia that in order to keep our office functioning we had to charge a monetary fee, even if it were only a few cents!"

His eyes were staring into the distance and he had clearly returned to his early days of practicing medicine.

"Yes, those were good days, even if we had very few possessions and very little time to spend together. We were so in love, and so happy just to be married and sharing a common love: medicine.

"But that was a long time ago, and this is now. Nothing good ever seems to last, you know."

"What happened?" I could not help but ask. I had to persuade him to finish the story. Some of the pieces of this complex man were beginning to fit together, yet there was so much more I wanted to know.

"I've said too much already. I promised myself I would put the past behind and get on with my life. Working here in the Iowa territory has helped me forget about my sorrow and concentrate on the needs of others."

"Sometimes talking about those things that are still painful helps the healing process...sort of like lancing the wound."

I was determined to do what I could to help him deal with the torment of the past.

"It was all so unnecessary!" he burst out. "I could have saved her if I had been there instead off treating some other man's wife!"

"What happened to Julia?" I asked gently, hoping the telling of the story might help ease the pain.

"The third year of our practice Julia became pregnant. Although she had hoped to practice a bit more before beginning a family, we were both excited at the prospect of having a child." Just then Dr. Jones turned abruptly to look at me.

"Have you ever had any children Rebecca? I don't remember seeing any the day I stopped at your cabin, and since I have never personally delivered any babies for you, I assumed it was just you and your husband."

"No," I said, his words like a knife twisting in my heart. "I have never had a child." I longed to ask him if he could shed some light on my inability to conceive, but I sensed he needed to finish his story.

"I almost did," he said with a catch in his voice. "A beautiful little girl, just like her mother. But God had other ideas!"

"Please tell me about her!"

"It was the middle of January, and a blizzard was raging. There was a knock on our door and as I opened it, a man stumbled into the office. He was covered with snow and looked to be frost-bitten. He begged me to follow him, saying his wife was about to deliver a child and he didn't know what to do. I asked him if she had been having any specific problems and he said no, but that she was screaming and he promised to get a doctor.

"I struggled with the decision I had to make. I knew Julia was due to deliver as well, and I hated leaving her, especially in the middle of a blizzard. On the other hand, I had taken the Hippocratic Oath and felt obligated to go with the man.

"I checked on Julia and she assured me she would be fine. There had been no contractions, and even if there had been, she reminded me that she was also a doctor and knew all about childbirth.

"So I went with this man to his wife, only to find that she had already delivered the baby and was doing well. There had been a mid-wife in the neighborhood and when the woman's neighbors had heard her screams, they sent for the mid-wife, assuming the child was ready to deliver.

"I felt obligated to examine the woman, if nothing more than to assure her husband that everything was in order. By the time I could prepare to leave, the blizzard was much worse. I knew it would be nearly impossible to find my way back home with the swirling snow drifting deeper by the minute. The man and wife persuaded me to spend the night with them and wait until daylight to journey home.

"Even though I had reservations about staying, I decided they were probably right, as my wife and baby would have a tough time if I were to die in a snowstorm. If only I had not let them talk me into staying, my Julia would still be alive!" His fist pounded the seat of the buggy with such force that the horses were startled.

"Thee had no way of knowing that at the time," I felt compelled to say. "We all make choices in our lives that may later seem foolish. I believe when we have tried to use our best judgement in making those decisions, we cannot look back with regrets. Can thee tell me what happened to Julia and the baby?"

"Julia had gone into labor shortly after I left and the baby was in the breech position. Instead of the feet being in the birth canal, however, the buttocks were positioned to come first. There was no way for the baby to emerge unless it was turned, which of course Julia knew because of her training. Using a mirror and forceps, she tried to turn the baby and in the process ruptured an artery and died within minutes, probably while the baby was yet alive. When I returned home the next day, my precious Julia was gone, lying in a pool of blood. But the saddest part of all was that she had nearly been successful in turning the baby for delivery. I lost everything that mattered to me that day, and I suppose I have never been the same since."

The depth of sorrow in his voice was so great I felt I was sharing in his wife's death. I was not ashamed of the tears I felt on my cheeks, and now I understood why he had been so harsh with me when Betty's child had been a breech birth also.

"I knew I could never practice medicine again in the office where I lost my wife and child, so as soon as they were properly buried I packed up my equipment and a few articles of clothing and headed west. I managed to get to the Mississippi and take a steamer to Burlington where my sister lived. After a time of rest, I started walking and vowed to stop at the first settlement that needed a doctor. That turned out to be Salem, and I've been here ever since. Ten years now, to be exact."

I was at a loss for words. I felt like I needed to comfort him, yet he seemed to have dealt with his loss in his own way.

"I would appreciate it if you would not repeat what I have just told you to anyone. I have tried very hard to make work my top priority and that has helped me a great deal. I know some folks out on the prairie think I'm too short with them, but I suppose that's just my way. Julia used to chide me about my bedside manner, telling me I was a grouchy old bear at times. I just told her I thought she was too kind-hearted and got too involved in her patients' problems. Then we would laugh about it and continue with our own approaches. I don't believe one can change the way they are, do you?"

I wasn't sure if he wanted me to answer, but I sensed an opportunity to witness to this man who had been through so much.

"Actually, I do believe a person can change, although their basic personality may remain constant. I believe that when one has a personal relationship with God, He can work in that person's soul and change their attitudes about things. In the seventeenth verse of Second Corinthians Paul says, "Therefore, if anyone is in Christ, he is a new creation; the old is gone, the new has come!"

"Well, I don't put much stock in religion. I know you Quakers have some strange ways and I respect your right to believe what you want. I believe in God in my own way. I do believe He exists, having worked with the human body as much as I have. It's just too miraculously constructed to be an act of nature. Now that personal stuff...well, I think I'll just leave that to you religious folks."

Sensing anything more I might say on the subject would only make matters worse, I chose to remain silent. One thing was clear, however: I would have to put Dr. Jones on my prayer list. Now why had I not thought of doing that before?

When we arrived back at Salem that day, it was my attitude that had been changed. I viewed Dr. Jones in a whole different light, and it made working with him much more pleasant.

When my month of training was over, I marveled at the things I had learned from this man. He had kept his promise to loan me his medical books, and I had taken at least one back to the hotel room each night. Some nights I could only get a few pages read before sleep claimed my weary body, while other times I would read far into the night trying to soak up as much knowledge as possible during my short stay.

The real lessons, however, were learned at his practice. I learned the positions of the bones in the body so as to know how to realign them when broken. Dr. Jones let me set a broken arm and finger and declared I didn't need leg practice since I had set father's broken leg when I was sixteen. I told him I did not really think I could remember how it was done, but he assured me that once you had set a bone it was something you would not forget.

I became an expert at stitching wounds, probably from the many hours of quilting and patchwork I had done as a child. I became so good at it, in fact, that Dr. Jones would insist that I do any lacerations that needed stitching. There was only one operation during the month, the removal of an elderly woman's gall bladder. Even Dr. Jones was amazed at the size of the gall stones, some being as large as marbles. He made sure I understood surgery was not something I should ever attempt, unless, of course, the person was in immediate danger of passing on. I told him he need not worry about me trying to do any surgeries!

My biggest joy, however, had been in assisting with the births of three babies during our time together. Though each had been relatively simple, I was continuing to learn more and more about childbirth. I felt my biggest strength in this area was knowing how to comfort the often distraught mothers. I could almost feel their pain, while at the same experience their joy when the baby finally took its first breath. I no longer felt the intense grief of having no children of my own, and in a sense I felt these babies were in a small way mine, too.

When Joshua arrived to pick me up at our appointed time, it was with a bit of sadness that I left my home of over a month. Of course it was wonderful to see my husband again, even though he had managed to make several trips to Salem for various reasons (some of which I was sure he invented!) during my stay there.

I wanted to ask Dr. Jones what he expected of me now, but I was not certain if it would be appropriate for me to ask. I was relieved, then, when he told me he had already spoken to several of the families living near our farm. He had wanted to let them know I was trained in some of the simple procedures of medicine and could be called upon for assistance as opposed to riding all the way to Salem for him.

As we were preparing to leave for home, Dr. Jones (I never had felt comfortable calling him Charles!) came and shook my hand.

"This has worked out far better than I anticipated, Rebecca." Then, turning to my husband he said, "You have a remarkable wife, Joshua, I hope you appreciate her!"

"Oh I do, Dr. Jones; believe me, I do!"

"Take care, Rebecca, and I will expect a report on all your cases every few weeks. If you need any supplies, either send word to me, or stop by the office when you are in town. I know I am going to enjoy the extra freedom your help will provide me!"

"How can I ever thank thee for all thee has taught me?" I asked. "I will try not to disappoint thee!"

"You will do just fine, young lady. Now get home and spend some time with that husband of yours!"

"I thank thee, Doctor," Joshua called as he started the horses down the street. "Please stop by for a meal when you are out our way! Our door is always open!"

"Thank you! I'll do that sometime!"

And somehow, I had the feeling he would!

8

Acceptance

Disappointed. That was the only word to describe how I felt in the weeks following my training with Dr. Jones. I suppose it was in part due to my unrealistic expectations. I had hoped to be busy within the neighborhood, tending minor injuries, if nothing else. When the first month passed with not a single request for my services, I was so disappointed my mood was clearly felt by Joshua.

"Rebecca, would thee like to visit the Johnsons or thy mother today?" he would say, knowing I needed to do something besides stay at home and wait to be summoned.

"No," I would reply, "I think it would be best if I just finished my work here at home today."

Finally, Joshua could no longer contain his concern. "Rebecca," he said gently one morning after our chores were finished, "Thee needs to quit sitting in this cabin day after day! Thee has mended every stitch of clothing I own, some of which did not even need repair!"

"I was practicing my stitching to use when someone comes with a laceration," I said stiffly.

"Rebecca, thee is the best seamstress I know! Surely thee does not need to practice each and every day to remember how to use the needle and thread!"

"Please, Joshua, leave me in peace. Have I not taken good care of our home? Do I not provide for thy meals? Do I not spend many hours in the garden and with the livestock? If thee is not satisfied with my work, please say so."

"Rebecca, thee knows I admire thy work. Thee works as hard as any woman I know. But there is only thee and me, and there are better ways to spend thy time than sitting in this cabin day after day!"

"I had thought I would have the opportunity to put to use what I learned with Dr. Jones," I said bitterly. "But for some reason I am not being called upon."

"Rebecca, I cannot think of one family in this area that has been in need of medical attention in the past month. Can thee?"

"I do not **know** everyone in the area, Joshua. Does thee?"

"I know most of them. Thee must be patient. It may take time for some people to accept thee as a medical aide. I am certain once they see the kind of work thee does, they will be anxious for thy help. In the meantime, I think thee should go back to thy regular visits with Betty and thy mother."

"Joshua," I said, pondering his words, "has thee heard something about my abilities thee has not told me? Are there those who believe I cannot adequately meet their medical needs?"

I could tell by the look of concern on his face that he had indeed heard something he had not wanted to tell me.

"I am going to share this with thee, but I want thee to promise not to think harshly of the person."

"What is it?" I asked, not knowing if I really wanted to know what was being said.

"Does thee remember Joseph Roberts and his family? They live some five miles north of the Meeting House."

"Yes, I believe Mrs. Roberts attended meeting for a few months, though I do not remember seeing her husband."

"That is because Joseph never came to meeting. It seems he does not believe in God after losing his child in a hunting accident in Illinois. He moved to Iowa hoping to forget the agony of shooting his own son."

"He shot his son??" I asked in disbelief. "How could that have happened?"

"They were hunting deer and his son, who was only ten at the time, got disoriented and began to wander in the area his father hoped to spot a deer. When Joseph saw movement and what appeared to be a deer behind an area of dense timber cover, he fired."

"Only to discover it was actually his son he had shot," I finished. "How horrifying! I can understand his bitterness."

"Regardless, he had no right to say the things he said about thee!"

Now I knew it must have been something slanderous for Joshua to react so strongly. "Just tell me, Joshua. I can not work on the problem unless I know exactly what it is!"

"While thee was with Dr. Jones, there was a cabin raising for the Groves family. Joseph Roberts was one of the men who came to help. When someone mentioned you were working with Dr. Jones, he became quite loud. He said women should keep their places, in the home, and let men do the doctoring. He said he would never trust a woman to treat any of his family!"

"And what was the response of the others?" I asked quietly.

"A few of them nodded, but most remained silent. I thought most of them knew thee and would ignore his words. Apparently I was wrong. Perhaps they were only silent because I was present. I am sorry, Rebecca, I only wish they knew thee the way I know thee. Then they would have no doubts."

"I thank thee for sharing this with me, Joshua. I wish thee had felt thee could tell me earlier; it might have eased my mind. Thee cannot imagine the doubts I have had about myself. At least now I know a possible explanation for my lack of patients!"

"I still believe the main reason thee has not been called on is because of the lack of illness and injury recently. I know thee will be needed eventually if thee will have a bit of patience!"

"I think I will visit the Johnsons after all," I said, rising to leave. "I have not seen Betty—except at meeting of course—since I was in Salem. She is always good for my soul!"

A look of wistfulness crossed Joshua's face, but I chose to ignore it. "I shall probably stay until evening, if thee does not mind. There are biscuits left from this morning, and a bit of smoked ham in the cupboard for thy dinner."

"All right, Rebecca. I hope thee has a good visit with Betty. Perhaps she can shed additional light on thy problem."

As always, Betty greeted me with a broad smile and bear-like hug. "Rebecca, how has thee been? I have longed to know about thy training with Dr. Jones, but it seems I spend all my time making sure my family is properly fed and clothed. I will be glad when they become a bit more independent so I may do a bit of visiting myself!

"But here—I have been going on and on. Please! Tell me all about thy studies!"

I shared some of what I had done with Dr. Jones, though I kept my promise—and his story—to myself. I knew Betty would see him in a different light if she knew about his wife and baby, but I would not betray his confidence. I also told her about my conversation with Joshua and what Joseph Roberts had said.

"That is the most awful thing I have heard in a long time! I am surprised Luke did not tell me about it after the cabin raising."

"Perhaps he was just trying to protect both of us," I ventured.

"Luke knows I have no desire to be 'protected!' We have never kept anything from one another, and that is why our marriage is so strong."

"Then perhaps he was not in the area when Joseph gave his little speech. Whatever the case may be, I need to know what thee thinks I should do about the situation. I long to be of service to the community. But how can I be used with attitudes like that?"

"I do not know for sure what we can do, but I do know we are not going to stand around while vicious rumors are being spread!"

I could not help but laugh. "Oh my dear Betty! I do not really think it is a matter of 'vicious rumors!' Perhaps more a case of old-fashioned ideas!' "

"I still cannot imagine why someone would not want thee to treat their illnesses. If they had seen thee when Ruth was born, they would know thee was intelligent and compassionate, and deserving of their trust!"

"I think I will come to thy home more often!" I said with a laugh. "As I said to Joshua earlier, thee is good for my soul!"

"Luke and I will do our best to dispel any doubts our friends might have about thee. And if I have a chance to visit with Joseph Roberts, I will let him know what I think of his 'old-fashioned ideas!'"

"Thee has helped more than thee will ever know!" I told her earnestly. "I realize now there is one thing I neglected to do: trust in God! If He wants me to be of service to those around me, I am certain He will provide a way for me to do so! I will also pray for Mr. Roberts. He has gone through a terrible experience with his son, and we should be concerned for his soul."

After catching up on the other news and spending some time with the children, I rode home in peace. I had tried to be obedient to the Light, and now I would have to trust God to do as he saw fit.

———————

It was not long before God did indeed provide me with the opportunity to serve. It was nearly dark, and only a few days before Christmas. Joshua and I had been working with the cattle, making sure they had adequate straw for bedding and hay to eat. Just as we were making our way back to the cabin, we could see the outline of a horse and rider in the distance. It was Henry McCracken, a neighbor of the Roberts.

Jumping from his horse, I could see there must be some sort of emergency. "Rebecca Frazier...can thee come? My neighbor Joseph Roberts has fallen through the ice and broken his leg. He wanted me to ride for Dr. Jones, but the leg is badly broken, the bone sticking through the skin. It is bleeding something fierce, and I am fearful for his life."

"Did thee put a tourniquet above the break?" I asked, trying to remember the procedures I had learned.

"No, but his wife is putting pressure between the wound and the heart to slow down the blood."

"I wish thee had thought of tying something around the leg!" I said more to myself than Henry. "Is he in shock?"

"I would not know...what are the symptoms?"

"Is he sweating profusely? Is his skin pale? Is he chilling? Asking for water? Is his breathing labored?"

"I...I...I don't remember!"

Now I had to make sure Henry did not go into shock. "Please take me to him," I commanded, seeing Joshua running towards us with Samson and my medical bag.

"God be with thee," Joshua said as I quickly climbed on

Samson's back. "I will be praying for thee!"

Henry's anxiety was evident. He rode so fast I nearly lost sight of him a number of times. Fortunately, I knew approximately where the Roberts' farmstead was located, and within fifteen minutes we were in front of the cabin.

When I saw the trail of blood leading from the river to the cabin, I knew there would be no time to lose. There was a very real possibility of shock, especially with the icy cold temperature of the water. I hoped the only thing his family had done was try and get the bleeding stopped. If he were in shock, moving him could be a disaster.

I had spent the entire ride over trying to discern the best approach to take when I was finally face to face with the man whose bitter words had continued to haunt me. What would I do if Joseph refused to let me treat him? What if his wife felt the same way and refused to let me through the door?

I would just have to do what the Spirit led me to do. Saying a quick prayer for wisdom and strength, I quickly followed Henry into the cabin. Helen Roberts had sent the children to the loft and I could hear their muffled sobs. They must have seen the injury, I thought grimly. Helen was leaning over the now still body of her husband, trying to keep him warm. She had piled several quilts over his shaking body: a sure sign of shock.

"Helen," I said quietly, "may I take a look at the injury?"

Startled by my voice, she turned to see who had spoken.

"Mrs....Mrs....Frazier! What are ya doin' here? I sent Henry to fetch Dr. Jones!"

"I know thee did," Henry spoke up in my defense, "but I was concerned about the loss of blood. It would have taken nearly two hours for me to get back here with Dr. Jones, and then only if I found him at home! I know thee would have preferred Dr. Jones, but Betty Johnson told my wife and me how good Rebecca Frazier was. I thought the emergency called for immediate action."

I soon learned Joseph was still conscious. Summoning all his remaining strength, he raised up on one elbow and looked directly at me.

"I will NOT have a woman treat this leg!" he hissed, "I'd rather die first!"

"Joseph, thee WILL die if the bleeding is not stopped immediately!" Henry spoke sharply. "Mrs. Frazier has trained with Dr. Jones, and I am certain she will know what to do!"

"Please, Joseph!" his wife begged. "She's here, and we gotta do somethin'!"

When there was no response, it was evident Joseph was now in shock and unconscious. Acting quickly, I pulled the quilts off the leg. The sight was something I had never before seen. The leg had bled through the several layers of cloth his wife had wrapped around it, and the blood was now soaking into the bedding.

When I could see the wound clearly, it looked like the bleeding had begun to ease. After washing my hands as carefully as I could, I began to assess the situation. The bone did not appear to be splintered; a clean break. That was one thing in our favor. I quickly located the torn section of the bleeding artery and managed to stitch it closed. All those days of practicing my stitches had paid off after all, I thought grimly.

The difficult part, I knew, would be getting the two ends of bone lined up. Joseph was delirious by this time, the pain and shock taking their toll. Quickly taking his pulse, I could tell his blood pressure must be dropping. I had to get the bone set as quickly as possible without further damage to blood vessels and muscle tissue.

Enlisting the help of Henry, who held the upper part of the leg, I finally got the bones in place—at least as nearly as I could tell. Working as quickly and carefully as possible, I cleaned and disinfected the wound before stitching the layers of muscle and skin together. I knew the chance of infection was high; I would have to pray the wound would heal cleanly.

My dress was soaked with sweat and blood; even my shoes and socks had splatters on them. Helen turned pale as she gazed at my appearance. I hoped she was listening as I gave her instructions on treating her husband's injury.

"I will send for Dr. Jones tomorrow if thee would like," I said calmly, expecting they would want him to come.

"I don't think we'll have ta do that," Helen said quickly. "I can see the color comin' to his cheeks, and his breathin' is more even. If we have any problems, we'll jus call ya ta come back!"

I must have done something right, I thought tiredly, wishing I were clean and home in bed. I quickly packed my bag, feeling confident Mr. Roberts was well on his way to recovery.

"I shall return tomorrow to check on the bandages," I said quietly, preparing to leave.

"Thank-ya," came the faint words from the fallen man on the bed. "I'm sorry," might have been more gratifying, but for now, thank-ya would do just fine!

9

The Split

I continued to visit the Roberts' cabin to clean and bandage Joseph's leg. The splint Henry McCracken had fashioned while I stitched the leg appeared to be keeping the bones aligned. Even though the wound was healing nicely, Joseph refused to acknowledge my presence. When I would ask him a question, he would either grunt or not respond at all. It was as if he were being held hostage by both his leg and me!

It was the second month before I felt Joseph was out of danger. As I prepared to leave for the last time, I knew there were things I wanted to say to Joseph, but I did not want to antagonize him further. When I was slow to depart, Joseph must have sensed there was something on my mind.

"Go ahead! Let me have it!" he demanded. "Tell me what an ungrateful fool I've been! Tell me how badly I've treated ya!"

"I have no intention of telling thee anything of the sort," I said firmly. "I know thee does not believe women should be doing the kind of work I am engaged in. At first, I was angry with thee for sharing thy opinion with the others at the cabin raising for the Groves. I felt thee did not even know me, yet were influencing others to form negative opinions regarding my abilities. I have come to realize, however, that my service is to the Lord, and if He wants to use me, He will provide the opportunities.

"I am sorry thee had to have the accident, but I am not sorry I had the training and ability to save thy life the night thee fell in the river!"

For once, Joseph Roberts seemed to be at a loss for words. I knew he had probably never had a woman stand up to him before. I had found his wife, Helen, to be one of the sweetest women I had ever met. But when it came to her husband, she did exactly as he said. I sensed she feared him, even when he was flat on his back in bed! How fortunate, I later thought, that Joshua treated me as an equal, respecting my opinions and abilities.

"Please take this ham and side pork home with ya," Helen said quickly as she shoved the meat into my arms, sensing the tension in the air. "It ain't much, but it's all we got to pay ya with."

"I could not possibly..." take your food, I started to say. Looking at the silent plea in her eyes, however, I quickly changed my mind. "I would be happy to have the meat, Helen. Thee is most kind to think of me in this way."

I could see Joseph scowling in the corner, still on the bed where I had first seen him.

Feeling more confident, I turned back to Helen. "We are still meeting at East Grove Friends every First Day," I said quietly. "We would enjoy having thee and thy family worship with us if thee could come again some time."

Helen's eyes lit up as she seemed to remember her past visits. "I'd sure like that!" she said, then, looking at her husband added quickly, "but I don't know if I can git the chores done in time now that Joseph is laid up. It takes nearly all mornin' to get the livestock tended to."

"Just remember that you are always welcome. Your

whole family is," I added, looking directly at Joseph.

"I ain't never setting foot in no church! What's God ever done for me? Let my own son die, He did, and now this accident. No, I ain't got no time for any God that does things like that!"

"I am sorry thee feels that way, but I respect thy right to believe what thee wishes. I imagine God might know how thee feels about thy son, however, having sent his own son to earth to die on a cross for the sins of all of us!" I couldn't help but say.

"Go home and leave me in peace," was all he could manage, turning his back to me.

Helen accompanied me out of the cabin, and though the air was bitter cold she had not taken time to put on her coat.

"I just wanted ta thank-ya again for savin' Joseph's life, Mrs. Frazier. He sounds kinda gruff, but he's been tellin' everbody that comes to visit how ya fixed his leg up and all. I wanted ya to know that," she finished, turning to go back inside.

I reached for her hand and held it for a moment, communicating the compassion I felt for this woman. "I will be praying for both thee and Joseph," I said, "and I am going to believe in a miracle where thy husband is concerned!"

"Thank-ya so much," was all she could say, but it was far greater pay than the ham and slab of side meat!

As the winter progressed, I seemed to have more and more patients to treat. Many were suffering from frostbite, and several had pneumonia and complications with influenza. It was difficult traveling through the snow, although the winter was milder than some in the past. I was enjoying my work, even though I knew Dr. Jones was still treating some of the families in the area. I continued to report to him on a regular basis, thoroughly enjoying our times together. He continually amazed me with his knowledge of the workings on the human body!

True to his word, Dr. Jones occasionally stopped by our cabin to share a meal with Joshua and me. On one such occasion we were interrupted by a knock on the door just as we sat down to dinner.

It was Mark Mendenhall, one of the young elders in East Grove Meeting. He appeared to be rather agitated, yet hesitant to speak what was on his mind.

"Mark! It is so good to see thee," I greeted warmly, hoping he would begin to feel more at ease. "Thee knows Dr. Jones, I believe?"

"Yes, we are well acquainted. Nice to see thee again, Doctor," he said, stepping forward to shake hands with Charles.

"How's that new daughter of yours doing?" Dr. Jones asked politely.

"She has had the sniffles lately, but she seems to be a healthy baby."

"Can thee sit and partake of the evening meal with us, Mark?" I asked, rising to get another plate from the cupboard.

"No, no, Rebecca, I can not stay long. There are several other members I must visit before returning home. I just wanted thee and Joshua to know..." then he paused, looking at Dr. Jones as if debating whether or not to continue.

"Perhaps I should be heading back to Salem," Charles began, before Joshua quickly interrupted.

"We would like for thee to stay," he said firmly. Then turning to Mark, "Please say what is on thy mind, Mark. Dr. Jones is a man to be trusted, if that is what concerns thee."

Looking from Joshua to Charles and back to Joshua, Mark finally began to unburden his load.

"There is trouble coming, Joshua, big trouble!"

"What is it, Mark, tell us!"

"We just got word from Ohio that there has been a split in the Yearly Meeting! Wilbur has forced Friends to choose between following his teachings and Gurney's! The meetings are in a turmoil and Friends do not know who to follow! It will spread to Iowa, I know it will! We cannot let it happen here, Joshua, we *must* not!"

By this time Mark's anguish was clearly evident and it appeared he had been thinking about the problem for some time.

"What does the Ministry and Counsel at East Grove recommend?" Joshua asked.

"That is what I came to tell thee," Mark replied, suddenly remembering his mission. "There is to be a called meeting of the Ministry and Counsel tomorrow at the tenth hour, and a called Monthly Meeting the following day at the same hour. I hope thee will be there, Joshua. I want our meeting to take a firm stand on this issue since we have no Yearly Meeting here yet."

"I will be sure to attend, Mark," Joshua said encouragingly. "I am sure the other members will feel the same."

"I thank thee, Joshua. I knew I could count on thee! I shall be on my way now," he finished, rising to leave.

"It was good to see thee again, Doctor."

"Likewise, Mark. I hate to tell someone I hope to see them again soon, my visits usually being prompted by illness or injury! But I do enjoy visiting informally with you Quakers!" Charles said warmly.

When the evening meal was complete, Dr. Jones seemed reluctant to leave. Knowing the ride to Salem would be long and cold, especially after dark, Joshua offered to let Charles have our bed for the night.

"I could never take your bed when it is the only one in the cabin!" he said firmly. "I might be persuaded to spend the night up in the loft, however, if you have no objections.

I always keep a bedroll in my rig in case I can't make it back in one day."

I almost felt guilty at the pleasure the thought of Dr. Jones spending more time with us provided. I hated for him to sleep in the cold loft, however.

"I am pleased thee will be staying the night with us, but I insist thee sleep in our bed. It will be easier for the two of us to keep warm in the loft than for you up there alone." As soon as I said the words I felt a warm flush creep up my cheeks.

I could see the amusement twinkling in Charles' eyes, but he simply said he would not consider sleeping anywhere but the loft.

Once the arrangements for the night had been settled, Charles began to ask Joshua about the Society of Friends. How we had gotten started and the basis for some of our peculiar beliefs. Joshua was very patient, answering his questions as simply as possible. When it seemed there was no more to tell, Charles asked the question he had obviously been wondering about for some time.

"How in the world did you get the nickname 'Quakers?' I think I would prefer 'Society of Friends' if I were one of you!"

I felt the need to speak to this question. "It is really quite simple," I began. "In our silent meetings for worship we wait upon the Holy Spirit for instruction and guidance. There are times when a person is so filled with the Spirit their body begins to quake. They then rise to present the message of the Spirit to the other believers present. When new members first attend, they are sometimes embarrassed by the quaking and find it easier to make fun of the believer than understand what is happening. Thus the nickname 'Quakers.' It is usually spoken in ridicule, and that is why we too wish to be known as the Society of Friends."

"That's quite interesting," Charles said, "and I must apologize for referring to you folks as Quakers in the past.

I simply did not know better."

"We are used to it," Joshua assured him, "and we usually assume those using the term are ignorant of its origin, as you were."

"One other question, if I may...can you tell me what your visitor this evening was speaking of? I assumed it to be something of grave importance from his concerned tone."

"It is a matter of concern," Joshua explained. "As I told you before, the Society of Friends began in England, but quickly spread to America due to persecution. We continued to grow in numbers as settlers spread up and down the Atlantic Coast.

"Being spread out, however, has its disadvantages. Meetings tend to be influenced by the leaders they have contact with. In recent years there have been two prominent leaders in the Society of Friends: Joseph John Gurney and John Wilbur. And although their heritage is the same, their beliefs are somewhat different.

"Gurney was born in England, though he spent several years traveling in America. Wilbur, on the other hand, was from New England and did not approve of some of Gurney's teachings. Wilbur felt many of the Friends of his time, especially Gurney, had sorely neglected the teachings of George Fox. He felt they were no longer a peculiar people, having conformed to the beliefs of other religions."

"There are those of us who believe Wilbur was simply envious of Gurney's affluence and culture," I could not help but add. "I personally believe Wilbur has done more to sow seeds of discord than any other one person in the Society of Friends!"

Joshua gave me one of his slow smiles, and I knew he did not completely agree with me. "Rebecca is not too fond of John Wilbur, I am afraid, so her support for Joseph Gurney is obvious!"

"Joshua, thee knows the reasons I support Gurney. He is for studying the Bible as a group of believers, being responsive to the Spirit's urging to carry the truth to others, and combating social evils. Wilbur refused to change with the times!"

"I would agree with thee on that, Rebecca. Both groups of followers believe essentially the same doctrines, the exception being the areas thee mentioned. The most regretful part of the whole situation is the discord which is being sown among Friends. If we are to have a positive effect on those around us, we cannot be arguing about which man is right and which is wrong. They are only men, after all!"

"And so now there has been a split in your membership, some supporting this Gurney fellow, and some supporting Wilbur. Is that correct?" Charles summarized.

"I am afraid thee is right," Joshua said sadly. "If Ohio Yearly Meeting has indeed split its membership, surely Western Yearly Meeting as well as Indiana will follow."

"That is one of the disturbing things about organized religion," Charles said seriously. "The inability to keep from putting men on pedestals. It seems to me that if your fellow Friends were looking to God for leadership instead of one of their own, this might never have happened."

"Thee is absolutely right!" I burst in, proudly.

"Yes," Joshua added, "as I said before, these Friends that are taking opposite sides essentially believe in the same things, that is the sad part!"

There was more discussion on the split, but eventually the lateness of the evening caused an end to our discussion. As I lay in bed thinking of the evening, I could not help but feel good about Charles's observations. Even though he claimed he was not interested in religious things, it was obvious that his soul was still searching for answers. For some unknown reason, I had the distinct feeling our doctor friend was closer than ever to believing the way Friends did. I felt like a burden had been lifted and I thanked God for beginning to answer my prayers for Charles.

I also said a prayer for the Ohio Friends, knowing the

turmoil they must be feeling, as well as for East Grove Friends. I knew the decisions our elders would be making in the following days might have a lasting effect on Friends in the Iowa Territory. And I wanted those decisions to be led by the Holy Spirit.

10

Little Concerns

When Joshua returned from the meeting of the Ministry and Counsel of East Grove, he was visibly shaken.

"It is not good, Rebecca," he began earnestly. "I had no idea there was such an even split in the Ohio Yearly Meeting. Nearly half of the members have chosen to follow Wilbur and leave the yearly meeting. I had supposed the number of his followers was similar to those he had in the New England Society of Friends back in forty-five."

"How many did he have then?" I asked curiously.

"If my memory serves me correctly, there were sixty-five hundred followers of Gurney, while Wilbur attracted only five hundred. Wilbur ended up taking his people and separating from the others, but he declared his group to be the 'New England Society of Friends!'

"What was the name of the original group?"

"New England Society of Friends! That is what caused so much discord. The larger body took Wilbur to court and forced him to change the name of his group."

"And now the same thing is happening in Ohio!"

"Yes," Joshua continued, "only now the split is almost an equal fifty-fifty. I can not imagine having to choose which man to follow!"

"Especially when their beliefs are essentially the same!" I said in agreement.

"Can thee imagine the turmoil that must be taking place in families? Some are even divided among themselves: husbands against wives, parents against children. How can we, as a Society of Friends, ever hope to influence the world around us if we cannot agree amongst ourselves!?"

"How do East Grove Friends feel about the division?" I asked, curious to know if there might some day be a split within our own meeting.

A smile crossed Joshua's face as he thought of the morning meeting. "I was so pleased with our group! We unanimously agreed to support both men and take from each those doctrines we think best further the Kingdom of God. Thee would have been pleased with the prayer time that followed, Rebecca, and I know all hearts were clear when we were finished."

"But there is one thing I wonder about, Joshua. Are there not some Friends who lean toward the teachings of Gurney and some toward those of Wilbur?"

"I am certain there are, but when the clerk opened the meeting, he made it clear this would not be a debate of the two men, merely a discussion of the direction East Grove Friends would take. The Spirit was in the midst of the meeting, Rebecca, and it was a joy to see men's hearts in agreement."

"What about the women's group?" I remembered to ask. "What was their feeling?"

"That is the wonderful part, Rebecca! When we came together to share our positions, the women felt exactly the same as the men. We do not want to follow men, only God!"

"I hope this will prevent a future split in Iowa. Of course, we have not even set up a yearly meeting here, so perhaps it will not be as difficult a problem."

"It is hard to predict what will happen in the future. If the Wilburites, as they are being called by many, choose to move westward again—like they did after the New England split—then there is a real possibility some will undoubtedly move to Iowa and try to sustain a following here.

"Mark has heard of two families who support Wilbur living north of here in the Springdale area. He believes they are already planting seeds of discord among Friends there. All I know, Rebecca, is that we must be diligent in prayer on the matter, and remain firm in our position as a meeting."

"That may be easier said than done, especially if some of the Wilburites are powerful speakers! I wonder if Abigail and Daniel know of any of these troublesome Friends in their area?" I mused. "I must remember to ask her the next time I write.

"Which reminds me, Joshua...does thee remember thy promise to me that we would visit my sister and her new husband? It has been nearly a year since they were married, and we have yet to set foot in their new home!"

"I have not forgotten my promise, Rebecca. But has thee forgotten thy work with Dr. Jones? When would we have had time to travel to thy sister's?"

"Thee is right," I agreed, "but that does not mean we can not prepare for a visit, perhaps during the summer. If we plan ahead, I can make sure our neighbors know I will be gone. I can also make sure Charles knows I will not be available for a few days."

"I think thee can plan to do that," Joshua replied. "In fact, I think I would enjoy a few days away from the farm. I imagine thy brother Jacob would tend the livestock while we are absent."

"Did I tell thee Mother's news the last time I visited her?"

Joshua's puzzled look was proof I had indeed forgotten to share this piece of information with him.

"Mother is certain Jacob is interested in a Friend from Salem. She said he had been so cheerful after the last quarterly meeting that she was certain something had happened. But thee knows Jacob! He would never say anything. Ever since that time he has volunteered to go to Salem whenever Father needs repairs or supplies, and last week he asked permission to stay overnight at a friend's house and worship with the Salem Friends.

"When Mother asked where he would be staying, he gave her the name of one of the prominent families in the meeting, the Stantons. She supposed they were a family he knew from Quarterly Meeting, but I remembered they had a daughter a few years younger than Jacob!

"Mother, of course, chose to keep silent on the subject. She knows Jacob would be unwilling to discuss his relationship—if indeed there is such a thing—with her or any other family member.

"On the other hand, thee, my dear husband, has a good relationship with my brother. It would not be too difficult for thee to ask him about the last quarterly meeting, which just might lead to a discussion of this young woman!"

Joshua gave me one of those, "not on your life" looks and firmly threw cold water on my suggestion.

"I will not do any such thing, Rebecca! Your brother and I have a good relationship because of the fact that I respect his privacy! If Jacob wants to discuss a woman with me, he will have to do so of his own accord! I am surprised at thee, Rebecca Frazier! If I did not know thee better, I would think thee was trying to be a matchmaker!"

"Oh Joshua, thee knows I just want Jacob to be happy. He works night and day with Father and has little time for himself. I just believe it is time for him to have a family of his own!"

"I will keep my ears open," Joshua promised, "and if there is anything suspicious in our conversation, I will try and see what I can discern from his words!"

"Thank thee, Joshua. I knew I could count on thee!"

Joshua gave me a look of resignation as he rose to leave. "I have much to do, Rebecca, and as much as I enjoy talking with thee, it is getting late and I must tend to the livestock. I am certain I will have to chop the ice again to get water for them, so it will take most of the afternoon. Perhaps I can shoot a rabbit or squirrel on one of my treks to and from the river. It would certainly taste good, although my stomach has been churning a great deal lately. I must be getting old!" he finished with a laugh.

"That reminds me, I need to do some churning myself!" I chuckled. "We are nearly out of butter and this morning's cream is just waiting for the paddle!"

"Happy churning," Joshua called as he quickly opened and closed the door. A blast of cold air reminded me of the need to bring in more firewood as well. It was certainly true—the work of a homesteader was never finished!

A snowstorm, the first major one since the first month, struck the last week of the third month. Joshua had to tie a rope from the cabin to the calf shed to negotiate the six-foot drifts. It was impossible to forge our way to the creek for water, so Joshua built a fire to melt snow for us as well as the animals. It was a long and tedious job lasting well into the night. I was relieved when Joshua finally staggered through the door.

"Joshua," I said anxiously as he wearily removed his wraps, "I was worried about thee! It surely does not take thee half a day to tend the livestock!"

He then proceeded to tell about melting the snow for water and how he had struggled to keep the fire burning, the blowing snow making the task arduous.

"Thee must be famished!" I said with worry. "I have

kept the rabbit stew warm for thee near the fire."

"I am sorry, Rebecca, but I do not feel like eating this evening. Perhaps I will be able to take some of it in the morning. It certainly smells good," he added quickly, as if his refusal was a reflection on my cooking!

"Joshua, I am worried about thee! Thee does not eat regularly, and when thee has done more than a day's work, thy body must be in need of nourishment. Is thy stomach still bothering thee?" I asked with concern.

"Now Rebecca, as I told thee before, when a person gets older their digestive system does not always work as it should. It was probably something I ate that did not agree with me."

"I think thee should have Charles examine thy stomach and see if he has any remedies thee might take. A man in his late twenties should not be experiencing the kind of difficulties thee has been having!"

"So it is 'Charles' now, is it?" he teased. "Thee has always referred to him as 'Dr. Jones' in the past!"

Blushing, I quickly replied, "I know him much better now than in the past, and I feel comfortable calling him by his given name. Thee knows Friends have always refused to use titles when referring to others!" I finished lamely.

"I do not believe 'Doctor' is quite the same as Mister or Mistress!" Joshua teased. "But I think it is good thee is finally using Charles's given name. Thee worked with him for a month, and we have had him in our home on several occasions. I have long wondered why thee always referred to him as Dr. Jones!"

As Joshua finished his words, a look of pain crossed his face.

"Joshua—what is it?" I implored, quickly moving to where he sat on the edge of the bed.

"It is nothing, Rebecca. Just a twinge in my stomach."

"Show me where the pain is, Joshua, please!"

Lying back on the bed, Joshua placed his hand on the

lower right side of his abdomen. I carefully began to apply pressure to the surrounding areas.

Much to my relief, I could feel no hard masses. I was still concerned, however, as the area to which he pointed seemed to be the place where I knew the appendix was located.

"I still believe thee should travel to Salem and have Charles examine thee," I said anxiously. "Where thee feels the pain is not thy stomach, Joshua, but the area of thy appendix. If it is infected, it needs to be removed!"

Joshua sat up and laughed. "Rebecca! If my appendix were affected, I would be feeling more than an occasional twinge! Does thee remember when one of the men on the wagon train from Indiana had an attack of appendicitis? He was in sheer agony! Rolling on the ground, in fact! My little pain is nothing compared to that man's!

"Does thee also remember," I asked soberly, "that he died before we could get him to a doctor to operate?!" My voice was now shaking and I knew I was close to tears.

Joshua rose and put his arms around me. "My dear Rebecca! I love thee so much! I am not going to die! Thee must trust me! I have too much to do to further the Kingdom of God before joining Him in heaven! But if it will ease thy mind, as soon as the snow begins to melt so I can travel to Salem, I will make it a point to have Dr. Jones examine me!"

"Please do it soon!" I begged. "I do not know what I would do if something happened to thee!"

"Nothing is going to happen to me, Rebecca! We are going to grow old together!"

As the weeks passed and spring arrived, Joshua seemed to recover from whatever had been causing his pain. The snow seemed to last forever, and once it had melted, there were many repairs that had to be made on the fences and out buildings. When I would ask Joshua about visiting Charles for a check up, he would assure me he still intended to go, but he had to get some of the work finished before planting season.

We both enjoyed the newness of spring. As the grass began to green, sometimes through lingering snow, it was a reminder of God's hand in our lives. The budding trees and new lambs being born were just what a soul needed after the weariness of winter.

I had not been called on to treat anyone for several weeks, and I was wishing someone would be in need. I longed to have a good reason to leave the farmstead after being inside most of the winter.

When Luke Johnson came riding up in the early part of planting season, I assumed he needed Joshua's help with some project he was working on. When he headed for the cabin instead of the field, however, I knew something must be wrong.

"Rebecca," he called as I hurried over to him. "I need thee to come. It is James. He has fallen and cut his head on a rock. I do not believe it is serious, but he is bleeding a great deal. If thee would like, thee can ride to the cabin with me."

"Samson is always eager for a ride, and it will only take a minute to get him ready. Thee can start back and see that James is lying down, and make sure pressure is applied to the wound to stop the bleeding."

Quickly turning the horse, Luke was on his way without taking time to reply. By the time I arrived the bleeding was stopped, though the cut was nearly two inches long and close to the temple.

"Well, James, I see thee had a contest with a rock and the rock won!" Although the boy was in obvious pain, he still managed a weak grin.

"Will thee have to sew it up, Rebecca?" he asked anxiously.

"Yes, James, we will have to get this hole in thy head stitched back together or thy brains might fall out!" I teased. "But I promise to do it as quickly as possible so thee can begin to feel better."

It was always difficult to stitch a cut because of the discomfort involved. It was especially hard for children as they had little ability to absorb the pain. James, however, was a model patient. Even though Betty and Luke were on either side, ready to hold him down if need be, he lay still. The tears running silently down his cheeks were the only evidence of the depth of his pain.

When I was finished, I gave him the highest praise possible, along with instructions for keeping the wound clean. He was not happy to hear he would have to remain in bed for the rest of the day, but I knew he would do as I asked.

There was not much time for visiting, but I did stay long enough to share my concerns for Joshua's health with Betty.

"I know thee is concerned, Rebecca, but Joshua is wise enough to consult Dr. Jones if he feels the condition is severe enough. I think thee is worrying needlessly, but I will remember to pray for Joshua—and thee, as well. Has thee been treating many patients lately?" she asked, changing the subject.

We then chatted a bit longer before I began the short ride home. Though I felt somewhat better after my talk with Betty, I still felt a nagging concern for Joshua. Perhaps I was letting my fears cloud my good judgment. As Betty pointed out, Joshua was a grown man, and certainly would make a point to see Charles if he felt the situation were serious.

I would put my energies into my gardening and spring cleaning once again. I must have too much time on my hands, I thought.

I went to sleep that night determined to engage in something more productive than worrying! Joshua's even breathing was a comfort, and I would have to trust God to take care of his health.

11

Springdale

True to his word, Joshua made arrangements for us to travel to Springdale late in the summer to visit Abigail and Daniel. It was the eighth month before the wheat and oats had been harvested, as well as two good crops of hay cut, dried and put in the shed. I was still concerned about Joshua's condition, though he seemed determined to keep the problem to himself. There were times when the pain was too great for him to eat, and times when I knew he was behind the cabin, unable to keep down the meal he had just consumed.

Although Joshua had never taken the time to visit Charles in Salem, I made it a point to ask him for his opinion on one of my consultation days.

"I know something is not right," I finished after explaining the symptoms I had been observing over the past few months.

"Well, Rebecca, there are a number of causes of stomach or intestinal discomfort. You said you felt no hard tissue when Joshua let you examine him, so it isn't likely that his appendix is the cause of his discomfort. And as Joshua said, when a person is having an attack of appendicitis, the pain is usually quite severe. There is a condition, however, where the appendix occasionally becomes irritated, which might possibly be the cause of his pain.

"There is also the possibility of an ulcer. You know ulcers may be located anywhere along the digestive tract. Is Joshua under any pressure? Are there too many demands on his life?"

"He is always trying to help various members of the meeting with their problems. He is also on the Ministry and Counsel of East Grove Friends. Thee knows about the split in Ohio. It has weighed heavily on his mind, although he was pleased with the way the issue was handled in our meeting."

"Then that may very well be the source of his problem. Just out of curiosity, what did your meeting decide to do about the split, if I may ask?" Charles inquired.

I explained the feeling of unity we had experienced in both of the ministry and counsels as well as the monthly meetings. Men and women alike had expressed the desire to support doctrines, not men.

"I'm glad to hear that, Rebecca. Your meeting sounds unusual. This might come as a surprise to you, but I have been attending the Salem Friends Meeting when I am not tending to the physical needs of the community. After my visit with you and Joshua last February, I found myself thinking more and more about the beliefs of your faith. I began to feel a need to become more involved with the spiritual aspect of life.

"I have seen more than one patient recover from an illness when I was certain they would die. As I told you before, I have always believed in a God, but a personal Redeemer is something I would never have considered until my talk with you and Joshua."

"That is certainly good to hear," I spoke warmly, smiling. I wanted to ask him if he now accepted God as his personal Saviour, and if he ever felt the movement of the

Holy Spirit in meeting. I did not want to push him, however, so I remained silent. If Charles were seeking more in his spiritual life, I was confident he would find what he was looking for.

"How has your practice been?" Charles asked, steering the conversation away from himself.

I told him about the patients I had seen, describing the injuries and my treatments.

"And have you experienced difficulty with any procedure you attempted?"

"No, thee was such a good teacher, it has been easy to remember thy instructions!"

"Well, I would like to think your ability to treat the human body was due to my tutelage; I know, however, that for the most part that is not the case! You had done all the background work at the library before you ever knew me. You have a gift for this work, Rebecca, and I'm just pleased I had a small part in guiding you."

The way he was looking at me was almost embarrassing. There was a mixture of admiration and...something else that I could not quite put my finger on. One thing I knew: whenever I was with Charles, he made me feel special.

"Who would have ever guessed thee would be saying such kind things to me after our encounter when Ruth Johnson was born!" I said quickly, hoping to lighten the conversation.

"I know I was too harsh with you that day. I hope you will forgive me for my disregard of your feelings!"

"Thee had good reason." I said softly, "Thy wife and child lost their lives in a similar situation. And as thee said, I was not trained to deliver a breech baby."

"Fortunately, that's in the past. I'm glad we've become good friends, Rebecca. You have been a bright spot in my life. A doctor has few friends, you know. People like to put doctors on pedestals, just as your religious Friends do with their leaders. I find it easier to keep a distance from my patients."

"That is one thing I will not have to worry about," I said with a laugh. "No one is going to put me on any pedestal, and I am glad of it. I would not know how to deal with that situation."

"Don't be too sure that won't happen, Rebecca. A person with the capability to heal the body gains a certain amount of respect whether they wish it or not."

"I will work hard to see that those I treat do not look upon me as something more than I am...your assistant," I said firmly.

Charles merely smiled as he prepared to leave on yet another call to check on a patient.

"As always, I have enjoyed our visit. Do you know when you'll be back again?"

"Joshua and I are planning a trip to Springdale in a few days. It will probably be several weeks before I will return to Salem."

"I'm glad to hear the two of you are going to get away from the homestead for awhile. That may be just the thing Joshua needs for his ailment. Have a safe trip, and I will look forward to hearing about your journey."

We said our farewells, and I returned home with a light heart. I was looking forward to the visit with my sister and her handsome husband. Hopefully, when we returned Joshua would be feeling much better.

Joshua had arranged for Jacob to stay at our cabin while we were gone. He would not say how long we would be away, only that I needed a good visit with my sister. Thee is the one that needs the time away, I thought to myself. The more I had pondered Charles's question regarding the pressures on Joshua, the more I realized how much he needed a rest from the worries of those around him. In the past two weeks he had been called away from the farm on five different occasions to handle various problems. He had also organized the cutting of hay at a neighbors' farm when the head of the house was confined to bed after being severely kicked by a horse.

Yes, Joshua was indeed under pressure, although he did not view it as such. "Why, Rebecca!" he had said when I asked him to get someone else to do the various tasks. "That is my area of service to others, just as your doctoring is to you." And that was the end of the conversation!

The trip to Springdale took two days. As we were using the wagon. Joshua wanted to take some extra grain he had raised to share with the newlyweds. We stayed overnight near Pleasant Plain at the farmstead of Luke Johnson's parents, thoroughly enjoying our visit with them. Luke's cousin was still excited about the opportunity to step right into a farming situation. He and Joshua spent the entire evening talking about crops and livestock and grain prices.

As I knew Luke's mother to be a wonderful cook, I took the opportunity to ask for some new ways of fixing the limited variety of meats we had. She was most gracious in sharing her secrets.

Of course she wanted to know all about her grandchildren and their progress. She was most concerned about James's head laceration, and I assured her he was doing quite well and she would hardly be able to see the scar the next time he visited. And of course she wanted to know about Ruth Marie, her only granddaughter.

"I just wish we could see them more often!" she lamented. "If only it were not so far to East Grove! It is difficult for my husband to ride great distances, so we must wait until Luke and his family are free to visit us. I surely hope they can find time to journey here before winter sets in!"

I felt compassion for this woman who had worked so

hard for so many years. She had been content with her life, and even now her only regret was that she could not see her family more often. Her gentle spirit was what I admired most of all. If only I could be more like her!

"Rebecca, thee does not realize what a tremendous person thee is!" Joshua said quietly as I shared my thoughts with him later that evening. "It takes a strong woman to do the kind of work thee does. A gentle spirit is admirable, but thee could not effectively work with the sick if thee were too emotionally involved!"

As always, Joshua brought out the best in me. He always seemed to know just the words I needed to hear!

"I thank thee, Joshua, for thy love. Thee deserves better than me!"

"I am the thankful one!" he said gratefully.

───────

The final leg of our journey went smoothly, in spite of temperatures hot enough to boil water! Even though Friends were not to exaggerate, I thought the comparison was accurate! Joshua seemed to be in excellent spirits, and I lifted a silent prayer of thanksgiving, believing God was answering my pleas for him to be healed.

"Rebecca!" Abigail called joyfully as we turned down the long lane to their cabin. She began running to meet us, quickly climbing into the wagon as soon as Joshua halted the now weary horses.

With arms around both of us, tears of happiness began to streak her dusty face. "I thought thee would never get here! Does thee know how long I have waited for this visit? Rebecca, thee should be ashamed of thyself for not coming to see us sooner!"

"Thee will have to forgive us, Abigail," Joshua teased, "but we knew thee would want to spend time with thy husband without extra persons around!"

"Joshua, thee knows better than that," she began to protest before noticing the ear-splitting grin on his face.

"Thee should know I would want to see my sister and her kind husband!"

"Rebecca has been working with the families in the East Grove area and even beyond, treating their sick and injured. She also has important meetings with Dr. Jones in Salem," he added, the twinkle still in his eye.

"Joshua!" I said firmly, feeling more than just the sun warming my flushed cheeks. "Thee knows my consultations with Dr. Jones are necessary if I am to be of assistance to him!"

"I know, Rebecca. It is just that thee has such a warm glow when returning from Salem. Charles must be giving thee wonderful words of praise!" he finished a bit wistfully.

Now I was really embarrassed. Had I neglected to notice Joshua's feelings where Charles was concerned? Could it be possible...did Joshua think there was something more than friendship between the two of us? No, my imagination was running wild again. Joshua knew Charles and I were colleagues, teacher/pupil at best. Surely he knew I would never be disloyal to him.

Putting my arm around Joshua's shoulder and giving him my most winning smile, I tried to set the record straight. "Joshua Frazier, thee is my one and only husband. I will love thee till the day I die!"

"I know that, Rebecca! Thee needs to learn to accept a bit of teasing from thy husband!"

Finally Abigail broke in, embarrassed to be in the middle of a husband/wife tiff. "Daniel would like for thee to meet him in the north pasture, Joshua. He has something he would like to show thee."

The look on her face was one of concern mixed with expediency. Now what could possibly be in the pasture that could cause that expression?

"I will drop thee off at the cabin," Joshua said, turning to me. "Thee and Abigail can catch up on all the news from the family and meeting. Then I will unhitch the horses and ride out to see what Daniel has in mind."

"Just be careful!" were Abigail's only words. That strange look again crossing her face. I would have to get to the bottom of this as soon as we were alone.

Abigail insisted on fixing us a cool drink of lemonade, having been to the store earlier that day to acquire the lemons and sugar. I had not tasted lemonade for many months, never feeling I could use our meager cash for such frivolity. I was annoyed at myself for thinking Abigail should not be wasting her money either. After all, Daniel had a much larger farm than we did, taking over his family's land following the recent death of his parents. He had also acquired other land as the opportunity arose. I would enjoy the lemonade and be thankful for Abigail's good fortune!

"This is wonderful!" I couldn't help but say after the first sweet, tangy mouthful.

"I am glad thee likes it! Daniel says it is too sweet for his taste, so the only time I indulge myself is when someone special comes for a visit!" she finished with a warm smile and gentle squeeze of my hand. "I have missed thee so much, Rebecca!" she said for the tenth time! Or so it seemed! I was going to have to be careful with the exaggerations!

"Tell me all about thy married life!" I implored. "Is Daniel everything thee thought when thee married him?"

"Oh, everything... and more!" she said seriously. "Much, much more!"

"Abigail, I have the distinct feeling there is something thee has not told me that is of deep concern. Is there something wrong with Daniel? Is he having trouble with the farm? Can he not get the work done? Does he expect too much of thee? Does he criticize thy work?"

"Whoa! Slow down Rebecca! Which of the barrage of questions does thee wish for me to answer first?" she interrupted with a laugh.

"I am sorry, Abigail. If I have been jumping to conclusions, please forgive me. But I do want to know what it is that concerns thee so."

Looking through the cabin door towards the pasture where her husband worked, Abigail began to tell me a story that would forever change the picture of Springdale I would carry in my mind. A story of courage, and freedom and hope!

12

The Challenge

When Abigail first began to reveal the secret she had been forced to keep for over a year, it was as if a great burden were being lifted from her soul. She knew she could trust me, as Daniel trusted Joshua with the same news he was sharing.

"Rebecca," Abigail began carefully, "Thee knows Friends beliefs about the Negro race? How God created all men equal, regardless of the color of their skin?"

"Yes, thee knows I feel the same."

"Does thee remember when we first attended Springdale Friends and Daniel spoke about his grandparents moving from North Carolina because they could not tolerate the idea of one man owning another?"

"Yes, I remember."

"At the time, I did not realize the depth of Daniel's convictions in this area. In fact, it was not until we were married that I began to understand exactly where those convictions would lead us!"

Now my curiosity was mounting. Abigail seemed nearly breathless as she considered the best way to break the news. "Rebecca, what does thee know about the Underground

Railroad?"

"Not a lot, I am afraid. I do know there is supposed to be a station somewhere in Salem, but I am not even certain it exists. Why is thee interested in the Underground Railroad?"

Abigail's eyes narrowed as she moved closer to me. "Rebecca," she whispered, "thee must not repeat what I am about to tell thee. It could mean the difference between life and death!"

Although I sensed she was being overly dramatic, the look on her face spoke more eloquently than the words she had just uttered.

"Rebecca, Daniel is running a station for Negro slaves in the north pasture!" she said in a rush, turning to look over her shoulder as if she expected someone to pounce on her for saying the words aloud.

The surprise on my face must have been evident, for Abigail took my hands in hers before continuing. "Rebecca, I know this is a shock to thee, but it is quite logical, actually. Daniel discovered a small natural cave in a cliff by the river that runs through our pasture. Knowing slaves often travel over water to avoid the noses of the tracking dogs, he thought the cave might afford a perfect hiding place while they waited for a boat to transport them further upstream.

"When he first mentioned his idea to me, I was adamantly opposed. I suppose my opposition was due in part to fear. I love Daniel so much, and the thought of him being sent to prison for breaking the law, or worse yet, attacked by slave catchers, frightened me beyond words!"

"Thee would have every right to be frightened!" I cried, finally finding my voice.

"Daniel was very patient, asking me to pray with him about the idea—never pressuring me or making the decision on his own. The more he explained his feelings to me, the more I began to feel this was God's will for us. And the more we prayed, the Light within became clearer and clearer."

"What about the Fugitive Slave Law? How does Daniel justify breaking the law?" I couldn't help but ask.

"I asked Daniel the same question. Thee knows how Father always stressed obedience to the law of the land!"

"Father has a lot of strong opinions on many subjects, Abigail. I was married to Joshua a long time before I realized Father's opinions were just that—opinions! He is our father, and we are to respect him. But that does not mean we have to agree with everything he believes!" I said emphatically.

"To Daniel's credit, he never once said anything negative about Father. What helped ease my mind on the subject was a passage of scripture Daniel read to me from the book of Acts. In the fifth chapter Paul writes about the time the apostles were thrown in public jail for preaching the gospel and healing the sick. During the night an angel of the Lord opened the doors of the jail and told the apostles to go stand in the temple courts and tell the people the full message of the new life they could have."

"I remember that passage, but what does it have to do with helping the Negro slave break the law?" I wanted to know, puzzled.

"When these men were brought before the court of the high priest, he asked them why they had gone against his orders. Peter answered, 'We ought to obey God rather than men! The God of our fathers raised Jesus whom ye slew and hanged on a tree. Him hath God exalted with his right hand to be a Prince and a Saviour, for to give repentance to Israel, and forgiveness of sins. And we are his witnesses of these things; and so is also the Holy Ghost whom God hath given to them that obey him.'

"So you see, just as Peter disobeyed a man-made law because it was in direct opposition to God's teachings, so we feel it is our duty to disobey this law which so clearly contradicts the teachings of the Bible regarding equality of men!" Abigail finished breathlessly, looking to me for approval.

"What thee is saying makes sense," I had to agree, "but are there not dangers involved in this work? Could thee not both be seriously injured—or even killed?"

A warm smile broke the concern on Abigail's face. "Just as Peter and the apostles were not afraid, Daniel and I feel we are serving a God who will protect us just as the angels protected the disciples in the Bible.

"There are times, of course, when I feel frightened. Especially when Daniel is gone overnight and I do not know when he will return. But each time I remind myself that we are doing God's work, and He will take care of Daniel!"

I began to feel a new sense of respect for my sister and her husband. Their faith in God and their willingness to help their fellow man was commendable.

"There is one other justification for our work," Abigail interrupted my thoughts. "Several months ago Daniel learned that many Yankee judges and legislators were restricting the master's rights of recovery, which made the law weak. Even when the more stringent regulations of the Compromise of 1850 were put into law, the Underground Railway has continued to prosper.

"This defiance of the law makes the Southerners furious, of course. Daniel believes they may even be willing to go to war in order to keep their plantations profitable with slave labor. It really is deplorable the way some of these black citizens are treated!"

"But how does this Underground Railroad work?" I wondered. "What exactly do you and Daniel do?"

Abigail then began to relate the details of their operation. The slaves would often come to the area where the cave was located in a wagon that appeared to be loaded with grain. "In fact," she said with a laugh, "a wagon that looks very similar to the one you and Joshua arrived in today! Only instead of being full of grain, the bottom of the wagon would house anywhere from two to six or eight Negroes. Usually they are young men, but occasionally there are women and children as well.

"When they arrive at the pasture and get the go ahead signal, they carefully leave the wagon and enter the cave. Of course, this is nearly always done at night to avoid being spotted by anyone who might happen to be on their trail.

"Daniel then helps them settle into the cave—at least as comfortable as one can get in the walls of a cold, damp cellar! I prepare food to take to them, and sometimes they remain for several days. Eventually, a boat with a hollow bottom arrives to take them to the next stop on the journey."

"And thee has never been found out?" I asked incredulously. "I thought the slave catchers had trained blood hounds that could track down the slaves and return them home."

"Sometimes they do catch them, and the pain they inflict is criminal! But if the slaves stay at the station they are nearly always out of sight, and even more importantly, they cannot be tracked by the ruthless dogs!

"The saddest part of the whole operation is the fear on the faces of these people as they wait for the boat. They often have no family, and no idea where they are going. They are putting their lives in the hands of white men— men of the same race as those who have refused to give them their rightful freedoms!"

"Are there other Friends who are helping these slaves? Or is it mostly white folks who sympathize with the plight of the black man?"

"Thee would be surprised at the number of Friends who have joined this cause," Abigail said with a smile. "In this area alone there are some ten families who help with the passage in one way or another. Sometimes they simply act as a decoy when the officials or catchers come asking questions.

"We Friends in Iowa are just helping a small number of the thousands of Negroes trying to gain their freedom. Has thee heard of Friend Levi Coffin?"

"Yes, Joshua was telling me of his work in Cincinnati a few months ago. I thought he must be some brave and courageous man to work on the Railroad. I had no idea my own sister and brother-in-law were engaged in the same mission!" I said admiringly.

Abigail smiled with pleasure. "I was hoping thee would not condemn our work. I had no idea thee might actually be pleased with it!"

"Thee is just as important as Harriet Tubman!" I praised.

"Oh Rebecca! I have done nothing compared to that great woman! First of all, she was a slave herself who escaped to freedom. I have had the comforts of a good home and family. I have known none of the pain inflicted on a slave!

"In addition, Harriet has made many trips back to the south to lead her own family and countless other slaves to freedom on the Underground Railroad. I can't imagine the courage of that woman! I can only do my part to right this terrible injustice!"

"I think thee is just as brave as Harriet because thee has more to lose than she did! She had everything to gain by escaping to the north!"

"But she didn't have to go back after her fellow slaves! That is what makes her so admirable!"

"I think thee are both brave, and both of thee are doing thy part in this work. Does thee really think there will ever be a time when men do not try to own others? I just think it is the nature of sinful man!" I said emphatically.

"There is growing opposition to slavery in the north, Rebecca. I am convinced all believers must become united in trying to right this wrong!"

"Now thee sounds a bit like Father!" I teased.

Abigail laughed. How I loved to hear her laughter. It

took me back to our first years in Iowa, back to the cabin loft where we spent many evenings together. We would share a story or humorous tale and burst into laughter only to hear Father's stern admonition to be quiet and go to sleep. She would always be my "little" sister, but she had grown into a wonderful woman!

Just then we heard footsteps approaching and the voices of the two men we loved. Though the tone was serious, their banter was light as they entered.

"And what have thee women been up to this fine afternoon?" Daniel asked pleasantly.

"Just catching up on the past year," I said calmly, looking at Abigail to see how much we were to keep to ourselves.

"We have had quite a chat ourselves!" Joshua said with meaning, and I got the impression they were not speaking of farming or the weather!

"Did thee get a chance to look at the river?" I asked tentatively, hoping to discover whether or not Daniel had spoken to Joshua about the Underground Railroad.

"Oh yes!" Joshua burst out. "Daniel has a fine storage cave near the water where he can keep things dry."

At that I nearly burst into laughter. Here we both were, two mature adults, trying to discover what the other one knew.

"Abigail told me about the project!" I burst out just as Joshua said nearly the same thing. Soon we were all laughing, free for the moment of the concerns we were feeling.

"How long has it been since thee has had any cargo?" I asked curiously.

"It has been nearly a month now," Abigail said quietly.

"That is one of the difficult things about this business," Daniel continued. "We are never certain when we will get a delivery. It puts quite a burden on Abigail as she never knows when she will have to suddenly prepare a meal. She is quite good at improvising, I might add!" his glance speaking volumes of the love he felt for his wife.

"Thee knows I like to prepare the various meals, Daniel," she said, returning the loving glance. "It is thee who must suffer eating the leftover portions when expected guests never arrive!"

"I did get a bit tired of venison stew that one month!" Daniel teased.

"He does not seem to be suffering from thy cooking!" Joshua exclaimed. "In fact, thee both seem to be hearty and healthy."

Though I knew Joshua was only teasing, I sensed an unspoken message flow from Daniel to Abigail. Now what was that all about?

Daniel soon answered my question. "We did not know if we should tell thee this or not, but since thee sort of brought it up...Abigail and I are expecting our first child sometime around the third month of the next year. We are both pleased and excited, although having a child will bring added risk to our situation!"

The tenderness with which Daniel looked at his wife ripped open the wounds of barrenness I had tried so hard to heal during the past few months. Knowing I could not ruin the moment for my sister, I desperately tried to swallow the lump that had formed in my throat.

As I looked at Joshua I sensed he too felt envious of the happy couple. Had Joshua wanted children as much as I? Had I been badly mistaken to think he was happy in a childless home?

"That is good news!" I managed, choking back the tears. I hoped they would believe mine were tears of joy rather than the bitter sadness I felt at that moment.

"Yes, thee will make wonderful parents!" Joshua added, quickly rising to clasp Daniel's hand and give him a quick embrace. Turning to Abigail, he did the same and again that wistful look seemed to cross his face.

We managed to get through the evening, though I knew

tears were close to the surface. When Joshua and I were finally alone in the guest room, there was no holding back the torrent of tears that quickly became sobs.

Joshua was quickly by my side, tenderly holding me, seemingly aware of exactly what I was feeling.

"It will be all right, Rebecca. I know the grief thee is feeling. I know thee has wanted a child for so long, and I understand how unfair thy sister's news must seem to thee!"

Joshua did know how I felt! How had he known? Was I that transparent? When the tears subsided, I finally asked him the question I had been afraid to ask for so long.

"Joshua, please tell me. Did thee want to have a family?"

"I have a family, Rebecca. Thee is my family."

"Thee knows that is not what I meant, Joshua. Did thee want children? A boy to carry thy name and work the fields? A girl to cherish and read stories to?"

"Oh my dear Rebecca! I know this will be painful for thee, but I must be honest in all things. Yes, I would like to have children some day. Most husbands want to share in the creation of offspring...there is a desire to nurture and teach that arises in men as well as women. I am sure it is a stronger drive for thee than me, however. Am I correct?"

"Oh Joshua, I have longed to have a child since the day we were married. I have watched Betty and Luke produce three children, the last of which I helped bring into the world. Others in meeting have had children and I know they will not be as good at parenting as we would be! Why has God kept us from having a child of our own?"

"I do not know the answer, Rebecca. I do know, however, that God is not the one to blame."

"Then who would thee like for me to blame? If thee believes God answers prayer, then why has He not given me this one thing I have prayed for all these months?!" I finished in anguish.

"When Adam sinned, Rebecca, the world was no longer

perfect. Because there is sin in the world, disease and death are a fact of life. Barrenness is another product of sin. I still believe God will answer our prayers for a child, Rebecca, if we have enough faith to believe His promises."

"I am sorry to say this, Joshua, but I simply do not have enough faith to believe God will answer this prayer. I have prayed too long and hard. For some reason God has chosen to bless other women, but not me!" I finished bitterly.

"I wish I could ease thy pain, Rebecca. I had hoped thy medical work would fill some of the empty places in thy life. I am sorry I have let thee down."

"It may be my fault, Joshua. In the course of my readings at the library I discovered that the inability to reproduce can be due to an imperfection in either mate."

"So that is why thee was always so intent on getting to the library every time we went to Salem!" Joshua exclaimed. "I should have known there was some reason for thy great desire!"

"I am sorry I could not talk about it with thee. I felt so inadequate. Other women were producing children for their husbands, but I could give thee nothing but a clean cabin and warm food!"

"I regret my silence as well, Rebecca. I felt much the same as thee...a failure as a husband! How much better if we had confided in one another!

"I do admire thy courage, Rebecca. Thee managed to be happy for thy sister when inside thee was feeling great pain. That ability to mask thy true feelings for the sake of another is one of the qualities that makes thee an excellent doctor!"

"I am not a doctor, Joshua. If I were, I would know what to do to solve this problem!"

"Has thee ever discussed it with Dr. Jones?"

"No!" I said emphatically. "And I do not intend to! I also implore thee to keep this matter between the two of us!"

"All right, Rebecca, but Dr. Jones just might know of a cure if we were to seek his advice."

"No!" I said again, more forcefully than before. "In fact, I do not wish to speak of this ever again! It is simply too painful!"

"I will respect thy wishes, though I believe some day thee might wish we had sought help on the matter."

I quietly turned down the quilts and slid into bed. I meant what I said, I thought bitterly. There is no hope for us, and even though Joshua did not believe it was God's fault, I felt quite differently. If God were a loving God, He would give me what I most wanted. Had not Jesus said, "Ask and it shall be given you, seek and ye shall find, knock and it shall be opened unto you. For everyone that asketh shall receive, he that seeketh findeth, and to him that knocketh it shall be opened?"

I had done all the asking, seeking, and knocking, but I had received nothing but disappointment, and hardly any open doors! No, Joshua might not blame God, but I did not know who else to hold responsible! As far as I was concerned, God had failed me in this area of my life.

It would be a long time before I felt comfortable asking for anything else from a God who refused to give me a child!

13

Trial by Fire

Our visit with Daniel and Abigail was a blessed time of restoration for both Joshua and me. Joshua was keenly interested in the "railroad business," as Daniel liked to call their aid to the Negro slaves. And although no passengers passed through the James' station while we were there, just the possibililty gave us opportunity for excitement.

I was content to help Abigail prepare large quantities of foods that could be kept for several days, knowing famished passengers could arrive at any time. Although it was still painful for me to gaze at my sister and know there was a new life growing within her, I tried to show some enthusiasm for my new niece or nephew. If I could not be a mother, then I would be the best aunt a child could have!

Joshua's health seemed to improve each day we spent away from East Grove. I was more convinced than ever that he did indeed have an ulcer and that getting away from the pressures of neighbors and Friends was the best treatment possible. Joshua still refused to discuss the issue with me, however. When I would ask if he were experiencing any pain, he would quickly assure me he felt fine.

At the end of two weeks, Joshua asked me if I felt it was

time to return to East Grove. I wanted to shout, "NO! We should stay here for at least a month for thy health," but I remained silent. Joshua interpreted my silence as an affirmation and began making plans to return home.

As we gathered outside the cabin the last day, there were tears in Abigail's eyes as we said our farewells.

"Thee will come back when the baby arrives, won't thee?" There was a pleading look in Abigail's eyes that I could not refuse.

"If thee would like for us to return, we shall try to at least come for a visit."

Looking to Joshua for support, Abigail then asked me the question that had obviously been on her heart and mind for several weeks.

"Rebecca, I know this is asking a lot of thee, but since thee is trained in childbirth, I wondered if thee would consider coming to stay with us for a few weeks before our child is due to be born."

Daniel quickly put his arm around his wife and gave his support for the idea. "It would really mean a lot to us, Rebecca, if thee would be present at the birth of our child. We both strongly believe in thy abilities, and would feel more at ease if thee were here!"

Now what was I to say?! I could never reveal my true feelings. They would not understand how assisting my sister deliver a baby—a baby just like the one I longed for— would be a form of torture. Fortunately, Joshua came to my rescue.

"I am certain Rebecca would have a difficult time planning to be gone for several weeks. This short two-week visit meant extra trips to Salem for our neighbors. Many of them even asked us to cancel the trip in the event an emergency arose and Rebecca was suddenly needed.

"Of course we will visit you after the child arrives— perhaps for a two-or three-day visit. That is all we can promise you right now."

I hoped Joshua could translate my look of gratitude. Abigail's crestfallen look, however, left me feeling like a villain! Could she not sense my discomfort? The thought of living with a pregnant woman, knowing I would have to assist in the delivery of her child was simply more than I could bear. Sister or not, I had to remain firm for my own well-being.

"I am sorry, Abigail. I know this means a lot to thee. I just hope thee will forgive me for not being able to commit myself so far ahead. And who knows—I might find my schedule to be light enough when the time comes to allow me to come up for a visit on my own!"

"Oh I hope so!" Abigail said, the warm smile returning to her face.

The journey home was peaceful, an occasional red or yellow leaf reminding us of the harvest season—and the vast amounts of work that would need to be done before the winter months were upon us. Some of the elderly members of the meeting were predicting a hard winter with much snow and cold temperatures. I was not certain whether or not to believe them as the basis for their predictions were squirrels and woolly caterpillars! Only time would tell if they were correct.

Joshua seemed to be particularly quiet as we traveled the now well-worn path back to the farmstead. He had been determined to make the trip in one day, meaning early departure and late arrival. I presumed his thoughts were of the many tasks he would need to undertake to make up for the time we had been gone.

I, too, was consumed with thoughts of the upcoming days. I wondered who had been ill or injured while I was away, and if there had been any births. There were two women in the meeting who were due to deliver sometime in the next month, and I hoped I would be able to assist them.

For some reason, aiding in the birth of a neighbor or Friend was not nearly as traumatic as the thought of being with Abigail when her time came. Why did I feel so strongly about not staying with her and Daniel for a time?

The answer, I knew, lay in the fact that I had always been a bit jealous of my sister. She had the prettiest face, got the best grades, and never argued or disagreed with our parents. She even got the man of her dreams and now she would have a child to solidify her marriage—as if it needed any help!

Recognizing the source of my despair, I quickly said a prayer in my heart asking God for forgiveness. I determined to pray daily about the situation and hope that God would change my heart before the baby's arrival.

It was after the twelfth hour when we finally arrived safely home. The cabin was dark, but smoke continued to curl slowly from the chimney. Not wanting to scare Jacob, Joshua called out before approaching the door. Before he could raise his hand to knock, the door burst open and Jacob warmly welcomed us home.

"I had a feeling thee might be returning tonight," he said excitedly. "I was unable to sleep, and when I heard the wagon, I was sure it was thee! How was thy trip? How are old Abby and Dan these days? Still happily married?"

Jacob had always shortened the names of those he knew well, with the exception of me. I was certain he probably remembered the fit I threw years ago when Joshua called me "Becky" because he knew I despised the name and he could get my attention by using it! Jacob had probably decided that shortening my name was not a wise thing to do!

"Yes, thy sister and husband are still happily married—and expecting their first child, I might add!" Joshua said, filling him in on the details. "Speaking of being happily married, what about that certain young woman from Salem, Jacob? I hear she is quite a charming young lady!"

Joshua's words surprised me, as he had never been one to tease Jacob. Even in the near dark, the look on Jacob's face told me there was some substance to Mother's suspicions.

"Freda Stanton is a fine Christian Friend. I am certain Mother has told thee all about her!" he said a bit angrily.

"I am sorry, Jacob," Joshua was quick to apologize. "Thy Mother has said very little about thee or thy friend, only that thee stayed overnight at the Stanton home some time ago. I did not mean to pry into thy private life. Please forgive me."

"It does not matter," Jacob said, turning to gather his things. "Nothing will ever come of it anyway, so what Mother thinks is not important!"

"As I said, I do not wish to pry, Jacob, but if thee would like to talk about the situation, perhaps Rebecca or I could help in some way."

"There is nothing anyone can do, Joshua. Freda's father is determined his daughter will have a better life than I can give her. He refuses to allow me to formally court her, although he does allow me to visit if I happen to be in town for a meeting at Salem Friends. The only thing he likes about me is that I am a Friend!

"I can understand his wanting more for his daughter than being a farm wife, but I am willing to allow her to continue her schooling. I have even told them I would leave the farm and go wherever she finds her opportunity for service. He says that would never work. Of course, he knows I have taken the responsibility of the family farm and that Mother and Father are dependent on me. But I would still provide for them, and I know they could get someone to till the land if I were to leave!" he finished, the anguish clearly present in his voice.

"Would thee object if Rebecca and I were to visit in the Stanton home? Perhaps we could help Freda's father see what a mistake he is making. But first I have to know for certain...does Freda have the same feelings for thee? I would not be in favor of a relationship that was one-sided."

The sting of Joshua's words was sharper than that of a bee, and I had never felt sorrier for him than I did at that moment. Had I cheated Joshua by marrying him even though my feelings were not as strong as his? I had thought I was following God's will, but his words made me wonder.

"Yes, Freda loves me in the same way that I love her. That is what makes it so difficult! I have been unable to think of anything else for the past several months. I would not be opposed if thee wished to visit her parents, though I doubt any good will come of it."

"We can discuss it again in the morning," Joshua spoke encouragingly. "Thee might as well stay in the bed where thee was sleeping. Rebecca and I will carry in our belongings and sleep in the loft."

"No, I will move to the loft," Jacob said firmly. "It would not be proper for a single man to take the only bed in the house while the owners slept in the loft!"

In no time at all Joshua had carried in our things and the cabin was once again quiet.

"Joshua..." I whispered after lying in bed for some time, hoping he was still awake so we might talk further about Jacob's quandary. When there was no response I presumed he had fallen asleep. I continued to consider our proposed visit with the Stantons. We would have to somehow persuade them of the wonderful opportunity they would be missing for their daughter if Jacob were not allowed to court her.

Just as I was about to drift off to sleep, Joshua began to moan and thrash about the bed. Thinking he was having a nightmare, I reached over to shake him only to discover his body was soaked with sweat!

"Joshua! What is it?"

"Oh...my side, Rebecca. It hurts so badly! Maybe thee was right! Perhaps my appendix really does need to be removed!"

"Roll over on thy back!" I commanded, quickly pressing the flesh for signs of swelling.

What I felt was unlike anything I had ever experienced before. A hard mass the size of a large egg could be clearly felt. I was not certain, but it seemed to be too high for the appendix. Whatever the case, I knew we must get to Salem and Charles as quickly as possible.

"Has thee noticed this lump before?" I asked quickly after calling Jacob to come down.

"Yes, it has been there for some time now. I just assumed it was the source of my discomfort and that it would disappear in time. I had decided on our trip back that I would see Dr. Jones the next time we had to go to Salem."

So that was what he had been thinking about all the way home. I was certain it had been a difficult decision, knowing all the work he would want to do as soon as possible.

"I wish thee would have told me about it sooner! I asked thee many times to seek Charles' opinion about thy condition. Yet thee never wanted to take the time to do so. Thee was always too busy with someone else's problem!" I finished angrily. I knew I should be more supportive, but I was afraid, as well as angry.

"I did not want to worry thee, Rebecca. Thee has had much on thy mind, especially with thy desire to have a family. There were also thy patients who needed thee." He seemed to be feeling a bit better, the pain subsiding for the moment.

"Joshua, there is nothing that means more to me than thy good health!"

"I know," he said quietly. "I sometimes wish thee cared

as much about ME as thee does about my health!"

"I do care about thee, Joshua! Thee knows that! I am thy wife!"

"I know that, and I am sorry if I have hurt thee."

Jacob came stumbling down the ladder just as Joshua finished speaking.

"What...what is it?" he stuttered, clearly having been awakened from a deep sleep.

"It is Joshua, Jacob. He has a mass in his abdomen and he needs to see Charles right away. Can thee drive us to Salem?"

"Now Rebecca, I am feeling much better. I have had these spells before, and they have always gone away. There is no need for Jacob to spend his time carting me to Salem when he needs his sleep. We will go in the morning, I give thee my word."

"I think thee should go now, Joshua!" Jacob said firmly.

"Yes, now!" I reinforced. "Thee should not wait another minute."

"No, I will not go until morning. Thee will both have to trust me to know my own body. I have promised to go tomorrow, and I will honor my word. Now if thee would leave me in peace, I would like to get some sleep!"

Knowing that when Joshua made up his mind nothing could move him, we reluctantly returned to our beds.

Sleep was now further away than ever. I thought of every medical case I had read about concerning the abdomen. I could only think of two possible causes: an affected appendix, or a growth of some sort. The appendix would be the best malady to have because in most cases simply removing it would take care of the problem. A growth, however, was another matter. Sometimes they were harmless and could be removed by surgery, but other times they were malignant, in which case there was little hope for the patient.

Why had Joshua not gone to see Charles months ago

when the problem first arose? Why had I not insisted he go? Was it because I was so consumed with my own feelings that I chose to ignore his symptoms?

No, I knew I had been genuinely concerned, and I believed I had done my best to persuade Joshua to seek medical attention. I had even discussed his condition with Charles, hoping he could shed some light on the problem.

Joshua was who he was, and I was not going to change that. He had made the choice to keep the problem to himself.

But what if it were a growth? What if something happened to him? Whatever would I do without him? No, I chided myself, I will not borrow trouble. We will travel to Salem tomorrow and know for certain the source of the pain.

But I could not stop the thoughts that continued to haunt me. Along towards morning I began to pray, asking for God's intervention in the situation.

But even prayer could not ease the gnawing fear in the pit of my stomach!

14

Healings

Jacob insisted on helping me take Joshua to see Charles the day after his attack. I was proud of my brother for standing up to Joshua in spite of his protests. It was evident that Joshua was trying his best to appear in normal health, but I knew by the pinched look on his face that he was still experiencing discomfort. Every time the wagon lurched he would look away, presumably to hide the grimace caused by pain.

———————

From the look on Charles' face as he examined Joshua, I was certain the news was not good. He asked a number of questions and Joshua's answers surprised me.

"How long have you been experiencing this pain?" "Almost two years now." I had no idea he had been feeling ill for so long!

"And what about the tenderness...I thought Rebecca examined thee several months ago and found no rigid areas."

"Actually, the hard mass has only been there a few

months—I didn't notice it until after Rebecca examined me that one time."

"Well, you might not have been able to feel the mass at first, but from my examination today, it is evident the growth has been there for some time."

How could I have missed the hard tissue when I examined him? Why had I not insisted on checking him regularly when I suspected there was a problem?

Because he did not want me to, I thought angrily.

"What does thee think it is, Charles?" Joshua asked tensely. For the first time in our married lives I detected a trace of fear in his voice.

"It's difficult for me to say for certain, Joshua. One thing I do know—your appendix is definitely not the cause of the pain. The location of the mass is far too high for an infected appendix."

"Then what does thee believe to be the problem?" I asked anxiously.

"I have only experienced two other masses like this in my years of practice. Both of those were growths that had to be removed surgically."

"And the patients were healed?" I asked cautiously.

"No, I am afraid in both cases the growths were malignant and by the time I removed them, the malignancy had spread to other parts of the body.

"Now...that does not mean this tumor is malignant. The only way we will know is by removing it and sending it by messenger to one of the laboratories in Chicago."

"And what will happen if I choose not to have it removed?" was Joshua's next question.

"That would not be wise, Joshua. If you choose to leave the tumor in place, it will continue to grow whether or not it is malignant. Eventually it will fill your entire abdominal area, preventing the lungs from expanding. In simple terms, it will suffocate you."

"When can thee perform the surgery?" I asked before

Joshua had a chance to come up with any more bright ideas!

"I would like to remove it today, if that's possible. The sooner it is removed, the better he will feel and the sooner we can get the results of the laboratory tests."

"I could not possibly get away from my farm work until at least next month!" Joshua burst out.

"Jacob will be glad to stay and assist with the livestock, and all our neighbors that thee has so willingly helped over the years will be thankful for the opportunity to repay thy kindnesses!" I reassured him.

Lying back and resigning himself to the inevitable, Joshua began to ask about the surgery.

"How long will it take?"

"That depends on the size of the mass and whether or not any of the organs are affected."

Knowing the significance of Charles' last words, I chose not to ask whether he thought there was more to the problem than just the tumor.

"Have you had anything to eat this morning?" Charles inquired.

"No, I did not want to risk another attack before making the trip in this morning. In fact, I have not had anything to eat for nearly twenty-four hours."

Had it been that long? Again I wondered why I had not noticed Joshua's lack of appetite. As I thought back over our visit at Springdale, there were several meals when he ate very little.

"That is good news," Charles told him. "The surgery would be much riskier if you had a lot of food in your digestive track. What I would like for you to do is spend some time with your wife, perhaps discussing the work she will need to make arrangements for while you recover."

"How long before I will be able to start working again?"

"With this type of surgery, it will be at least two months before you will feel like doing much around the farm. You should be able to begin moving about in a few weeks, but if you overdo it," he warned, "you will likely undo some of the stitches which would be a major setback. Now...are there any other questions either of you would like to ask?"

I wanted to ask what risk was involved in this type of surgery, and if there was any chance of his not making it through the operation. I decided to wait until later when perhaps I could speak with Charles alone.

"No questions, Doctor. Just do what thee must do so I can be about my business again!" Joshua exclaimed as he maneuvered into a sitting position.

"Very well. I have some errands to run that will take the rest of the morning. I should be back in time for dinner if you and Rebecca would like to join me. Of course, you can't eat or drink anything," he said, turning to Joshua.

"I think I will remain here and rest while thee and Rebecca have a bite to eat."

"I will stay with thee!" I cried, not wanting to leave him alone before the ordeal he was about to undertake.

"I would like a bit of time to myself, dear, and I know how much thee would like to talk to Charles without my presence! Please go and enjoy thyselves," he said calmly.

It was a bit disconcerting the way he read my mind these days! "If thee is sure thee does not mind my leaving thee..."

"Good!" Charles broke in. "I must be off, but I will stop back for you in about an hour, Rebecca."

Joshua and I spent the next hour discussing the details of what must be done on the farm and how to best handle the harvesting. We finally agreed to ask Jacob if he thought he could handle the livestock chores. Joshua then suggested we ask Luke to organize the harvesting of the corn when the ears had sufficiently dried in the field. He would speak to other Friends and neighbors. I was certain there would be a large crowd in response to the way Joshua had been a help to so many of them.

When the noon hour was nearing, Joshua asked me to come near the bed where he was resting. Taking my hand in his, he began to tell me of his love for me and the sorrow he felt for not giving me a child.

"It is not thy fault!" I cried, not wanting him to enter surgery in a poor state of mind. "Thee has given me more love than any woman deserves. I am just sorry I have not given more to thee."

The outcome of the surgery must have been weighing heavily on his mind, for his next words were fervently spoken.

"Please promise me thee will not be sorrowful if I should not survive the surgery. I am looking forward to spending eternity with my Heavenly Father. My only regret is that thee will be left alone."

"I wish thee would not speak of such things!" I said firmly. "Charles is an excellent doctor, and thee will feel so much better once he removes the tumor!"

"I have left the results in God's hands, Rebecca. Please do not misunderstand me...I would never want to leave thee and our mission at East Grove Friends. It is just that sometimes God's will is not always our will!"

"I love thee, Joshua Frazier. And I do not want to live without thee!" And for the first time in our marriage, I realized I meant each and every word.

"Thee has made me a happy man, Rebecca. I have waited many years to hear thee say thee felt that way!"

I leaned over and gently kissed him, knowing I was truly blessed to have him for my husband.

"Now," he said firmly, "go and have a good meal with Dr. Jones and give him all the wisdom thee has gained from thy readings!"

"Thee is speaking flattery now, Joshua Frazier! Thee knows Friends believe in speaking the truth in all things!"

"I was speaking the truth! I trust thee just as much as I trust Dr. Jones. I hope thee is planning to assist him in my surgery."

"I do not believe I could do that—unless it was an emergency, of course. I will stay with thee while he operates, thee can depend on that."

Just then Charles returned and we went to the hotel restaurant for our noon meal. I had only eaten there a few times while I was training with Charles, but I enjoyed the variety of patrons dining and the melodious sounds of eating utensils and voices blending together.

Our conversation was light, Charles sensing my need to concentrate on something besides the events of the afternoon. We spoke of our patients, and he told me of a convention he would be attending in St. Louis the next month.

"I wish you could attend with me," he said wistfully. "I know you would gain many insights into the latest medical techniques. Unfortunately, they only allow certified physicians to attend—a foolish decision as far as I am concerned!"

"Thee can tell me all about it when thee returns. I have always enjoyed learning from thee!" I said warmly.

Just then another couple came into the dining area and as the man turned into my view, I was shocked to see my brother Jacob! The young lady with him was smiling broadly, and I had never seen Jacob with such a happy look on his face! Seeing us sitting there, Jacob whispered something to the young lady and then they began to make their way to our table.

"Rebecca, Dr. Jones, this is Freda Stanton, a good friend of mine. Freda, this is my sister and I believe thee knows Dr. Jones."

Charles rose to shake hands with Jacob and ask them to join us. Sensing they would prefer to dine alone, I quickly reminded Charles there was little time before we must return for the surgery. After discussing Joshua's condition, Jacob and Freda both said they would pray for him, assuring me everything would go well.

"If thee would like," Jacob added, "I could come to the office after I return Freda to her home."

"I think that would be an excellent idea, Jacob. Your

sister could use some support."

"Then that is what I will do. I will see thee in an hour or so, Rebecca," he said.

"Thank thee, Jacob. Thee and I have much to talk about!" I answered, glancing quickly at Freda.

"I did not know your brother and Freda were seeing one another," Charles commented after they had moved to an empty table.

"Neither did I! Jacob just told us last night about this young woman, and he was certain her father did not want him to court her!"

"Perhaps he had a change of heart!"

"Perhaps...something must have happened considering the happy faces of those two!"

"Well, we should be getting back to the office to check on our patient and begin the afternoon's work."

"Charles, there is one question I have that I did not want to ask in front of Joshua. Just how much risk is there in this type of surgery? He will come through it in good condition, will he not?"

"I would not be honest if I told you there was no danger. Whenever you cut into the human body, you run the risk of infection. There is also the problem of not knowing what we will find in his abdomen once we open the cavity. But let's not think of the worst. I am confident Joshua will do well. He is a strong man, and also has a strong will to live."

"I never realized how much I loved him until I was faced with the possibility of losing him!"

"Unfortunately, that happens all too often in a marriage. It takes a tragedy to help us experience our true emotions."

"But thee and Julia shared a special love from the beginning, did thee not?"

"Yes, we did. But that made her death all the more painful. I will never allow myself to love another woman the way I loved her!"

Charles quickly rose to leave, obviously wishing to end the conversation. I felt only sadness for this gifted man who had felt such grief in his life.

Joshua was at peace when we returned and anxious to begin the tedious work that lie ahead. Charles quickly prepared Joshua, himself, and the area where he would operate. Soon the abdomen was open and the source of the problem exposed. It was so intriguing, and I had so many questions! I tried not to disturb his work, but there were some things I just had to know! Charles spoke to me as he worked, patiently answering my questions and showing me how to examine the other organs to see if the tumor had spread. When there was no evidence of that, he carefully cut away the growth and prepared to stitch the wound.

Joshua had handled the pain stoically, though he had finally lost consciousness toward the end. Jacob had been there to lend his support, though I found the surgery to be so fascinating I hardly needed anyone to hold my hand!

Charles carefully packaged the tumor which the messenger would pick up later that day. The surgery had taken nearly three hours, and the strain clearly showed on his face.

"It will be several weeks before we receive the results of the testing," Charles informed us, "but it did not look to be malignant to me. Of course I have not had a great deal of experience in this area," he cautioned.

"I think the two of you may as well return home. It will be several days before Joshua will feel much like visitors."

"I would prefer to stay with my husband," I said quietly, feeling my place was by his side. "Jacob, thee may take the wagon and stay at the cabin until we return."

"All right, Rebecca. I shall stop by home first to inform our parents of Joshua's surgery and my plans."

Turning my way, Charles began to thank me for my assistance.

"I did not assist thee!" I said with surprise. "I merely watched while thee did the work!"

"Ah, but you were of more assistance than you can imagine! Just answering all those questions kept my mind sharp. You forced me to speak through the procedures as I performed them, helping prevent errors. You were wonderful...I love your inquisitiveness as well as the ability to absorb information."

I felt myself blushing from the praise I felt I did not deserve.

Clearing his throat, Jacob excused himself and quickly exited the room. Charles began to clean the utensils as I took my place at Joshua's side.

Once again I began to pray for his complete recovery. I believed we had turned the corner and were on the right path once again.

"I thank thee, God," I prayed quietly, "for healing our marriage as well as Joshua's body."

And I thank thee, Charles. I thank thee for using thy God-given abilities to save my husband's life. And I thank thee for making me feel so good about myself.

15

Winter of Despair

Within a few weeks Joshua was feeling much better and was able to move around the cabin with only moderate discomfort. I continued to rejoice in God's blessing on my life, especially my newly found love for my husband.

I had also come to terms with my inability to conceive a child. I felt a calm peace in my heart, having turned the matter over to God, trusting Him to know what was best for Joshua and me. I had even decided to stay with Abigail and Daniel when the time for their child's birth arrived. Joshua had been pleased with the decision and assured me he would be able to manage the cabin on his own.

Jacob continued to ride over each morning and evening to handle the chores—at least when the weather would permit. It was turning into the type of winter the elders had predicted: cold and snowy. On several occasions I had struggled out to the livestock sheds to feed the hungry animals, but the snow was now drifted high in many places. I was not certain what I would do if we had a major blizzard!

The only dim spot in our lives was waiting for the pathology report from Chicago. Joshua and I were both confident the tumor was not malignant, but I knew the uncertainty was weighing heavily on him. Charles had been certain it would take only a few weeks to receive the results, but we were already in the twelfth month with no word. In this area, too, I was trusting God to meet our needs and continue the healing process in Joshua.

The new year, 1856, dawned cold and stormy with yet another heavy snow blanketing the farmstead. This time I was certain Jacob would be unable to travel on horseback for several days. I was determined to get to the animals, and Joshua was just as determined I stay inside.

"The animals will survive for two or three days on the hay Jacob left them the last time he was here," Joshua argued when I began gathering my wraps to venture out the morning after the storm subsided.

"Joshua, thee knows they need water as well as food. I am quite capable of building a fire and melting some snow for them to drink. The blizzard is past and the sun is shining!"

"The sun is deceiving, Rebecca. The wind is bitter—surely thee can hear it howl outside, not to mention the icy drafts blowing through the cracks. I do not feel comfortable with thee venturing out just yet!"

I was beginning to feel just a bit of annoyance at his persistence. I knew if he were able he would already have gone to the animals. I had waited a day after the storm subsided before deciding I could make it.

"Thee will simply have to trust me, Joshua Frazier. Believe it or not, I am a capable woman, and I am going to tend the animals whether thee approves or not!"

"Rebecca, thee knows it is not a matter of my approval. I am simply worried that something might happen to thee! Then what would I do?"

"Thee would manage," I said stiffly, not willing to give in to his request.

"I suppose there is no stopping thee," he said wearily.

"But thee needs to make sure the line is still tightly secured to both the cabin and the calf shed before thee ventures out. Please be careful to keep one hand on the rope at all times, and return as soon as possible."

I quickly opened the door, only to be greeted by a wall of snow so high I could not even see the calf shed!

"What is it?" Joshua asked when I seemed to remain fixed in the doorway.

"Oh...nothing to be concerned with. Just a bit more snow than I expected," I said, quickly closing the door behind me. A few feet of the rope were still visible leading off the cabin, but then it quickly disappeared into the deep drift. This was going to be a challenge.

Fortunately, Joshua had fashioned a pair of crude snow shoes while he had been confined to the cabin, and they were a great help in scaling the mountain of snow. It was tedious work freeing the line from its buried position, and soon I was sweating under the layers of clothing.

It took nearly an hour, as best I could figure, to travel the two hundred feet to the livestock. Fortunately, the snow right around the shed had drifted toward the grove of trees behind, leaving a nice working area. I quickly gathered some of the wood Joshua and Jacob had cut earlier in the fall and made a hot fire for melting the snow.

The process was tedious; each pail of snow would yield but a few inches of water, hardly enough for one animal. I fed the calves and then the hogs in the adjoining paddock while I waited for more and more water to accumulate.

My arms were weary, and I knew I had been gone from the cabin for several hours. Joshua would be worried if I did not return soon, yet I wanted to make sure each animal had been well cared for. Just as I was beginning to make my way back to the cabin, a strange jingling sound could be heard in the distance. I could not see over several of the drifts, but as the chimes got louder, I was certain someone or something was heading toward our home.

Moving as fast as the snowshoes would allow, I finally reached the cabin as the now visible sleigh came closer and closer. It was Jacob! And Charles?!

"Rebecca!" Jacob called as he caught sight of me nearing the end of the rope. "What is thee doing out in this weather?!"

"I might ask thee the same thing!"

"Thee should be in the cabin! Did thee not think I would come to tend the livestock!"

"How was I to know thee would have a sleigh? I knew thee would not be able to travel by horse for a few days, and I was concerned for the animals!"

"Hello Rebecca," Charles said quietly, obviously not willing to be in the middle of this sibling argument!

"Oh, I am sorry, Charles. Hello. I must say I am surprised to see thee!"

"Well, I stopped by your parents' cabin to check on your father. Jacob had mentioned to me when he was in Salem a few days earlier that Alfred was suffering with a cough and he was afraid it was pneumonia. Since I had the sleigh out to make another call, it was convenient to check on him as well."

"I did not know Father was ill! Why did thee not tell us, Jacob?"

"Father asked me not to mention it to thee. He feels thee has enough on thy mind with Joshua's recovery and all. I probably should have told thee anyway, but somehow I still have difficulty going against his word!"

"He is a stubborn one, I must admit!" I agreed.

"Anyway, when I saw Dr. Jones's sleigh, I asked if he would mind if I used it to come and manage the livestock."

"Then I have another question for thee...what was thee doing in Salem this time?" I asked curiously.

The color in Jacob's cheeks was from more than just the cold! "I was calling on Freda, if thee must know!"

"In all the concern for Joshua's surgery, I forgot to ask

thee what happened with her father. When Charles and I saw thee in the restaurant, we knew something must have happened for you both to have such happy faces!"

"It was a miracle, I believe! I had been praying and praying for Freda's father to have a change of heart. Then the day I helped thee take Joshua to Charles's office, Joshua asked me to bring Mr. Stanton to see him while you and Charles were at dinner. By the time Joshua was finished talking to him, he had agreed to let me see his daughter occasionally. I do not believe he is sure he did the right thing, but he has been very cordial to me ever since!"

"Joshua did that while he was waiting to be operated on?" I asked incredulously.

"He is a special man, Rebecca," Charles broke in, "and one of the reasons I came with Jacob was to speak with you and Joshua about a matter of concern to you both.

"Please! Let us move inside before we all freeze to death!" I said between chattering teeth.

"Look who I found outside!" I said as we all stamped to clear the snow from our bodies and feet.

Joshua was so surprised he nearly fell off the bed trying to get up to greet them!

"How in the world did you two manage to make it through the snow?!"

"Dr. Jones brought me in his sleigh," Jacob answered. "I think I may have to purchase one for us to use. The past few winters have been mild enough to let us manage with the horses. But this one is something else!"

"I would like to see the expression on Father's face when thee tells him of thy plan!" I said teasingly.

"I will simply not tell him! I have funds of my own to use, and if I have already made the purchase, what can he say?"

"Plenty!" Joshua and I both said at the same time! We all had a good laugh, knowing that at the sight of a new sleigh Father would indeed have a ready-made lecture on the topic of frivolity!

I quickly set about making us a late noon meal. Joshua had already put some of the cured ham and dried vegetables in the pot over the hearth, and I could quickly mix up some cornbread. This was certainly a pleasant surprise in the middle of what had started out to be a dismal day!

As we ate, I noticed Charles seemed to be in a somber mood. I was curious as to what he had to discuss, and I assumed he was going to give us some bad news concerning Father. The discussion around the table had been mostly of the weather and the misery it was causing.

Charles also seemed despondent over the number of patients he had already lost to both pneumonia and grippe.

When the dishes were cleared from the table, I felt the need to join the men and get to the real reason for Charles's visit.

"I must ask thee, Charles, what thee meant earlier when thee first arrived. Thee said there was a matter thee needed to speak with us about. Is it Father? Is he seriously ill?"

"No, actually your Father was feeling better when I finally got to his cabin. He should feel much improved in a few days if he will remain in bed as I prescribed."

Jacob and I exchanged a knowing glance at those words. Father was not one to stay in bed if he could help it!

"Then what did thee come for?" Joshua asked worriedly, somehow sensing the news had to do with him.

"I got the report back a few days ago concerning the tumor we removed from your abdomen." He paused, as if wanting to use just exactly the right words.

"And it was malignant, wasn't it?" Joshua asked quietly.

"I was almost certain it was not a malignant tumor!" Charles spoke in a voice that conveyed his troubled mind. "It simply looked like any number of growths I have removed in the past that were benign. I am so sorry if I gave you false hope!"

"But what does that mean?" I asked anxiously. "Thee removed all the tumor, did thee not? And Joshua has felt very well ever since the surgery! Has he not?" I finished, turning toward him.

"Yes, Rebecca, I felt much better after the surgery. But we knew there was a possibility the growth was malignant. I knew we could not fully celebrate until after the tests were back."

"So what does that mean?" I repeated, directing my question once again to Charles.

"I do not know for certain, Rebecca. If we were able to remove all of the growth and it had not spread, it is possible Joshua will recover completely. On the other hand...." he paused, considering the possibilities.

"On the other hand, what?!" I demanded.

"On the other hand, it may have been possible for a few of the infected cells to move from the tumor into other tissue."

"And if that has happened?" Jacob was the one to ask the question neither Joshua nor I could find the courage to voice.

"If that has happened, then new tumors may eventually begin to grow in other parts of the body."

"But how will we know if there are still malignant cells in his body?" I asked, cold fear beginning to grip my heart and soul.

"You or Joshua will have to wait until you feel another lump somewhere before you will know his condition."

"And how long will that take?"

"It's difficult to say. In most cases, it is only a matter of months before new tumors appear if the original area had spread."

"And if that has happened?" Joshua needed to know the worst possible situation.

"If that happens, you will probably have but a few weeks, possibly a month or two, before the tumors take over your body. But we will just have to wait and see. Let's not imagine the worst...your body needs your mind to see the situation in a positive manner!"

"So what are we to do in the meantime?" I cried. "Sit and wait for these monsters to appear?!"

Joshua could sense my growing despair, and sought to assure me. "We do not know that the malignancy has spread, Rebecca. This is something we must trust God to handle. Neither thee nor I has the strength to carry this burden alone. But God has never failed us yet, and we will trust Him!"

"I am very sorry," Charles said again. "As I told Rebecca when we were doing the surgery, I didn't find any evidence that the tumor had spread. I think that is a positive sign, at least."

"We will hold on to that bit of good news, Joshua," Jacob said encouragingly. "I think I will take a look at the livestock before we head back. I know Dr. Jones would like to return to Salem before nightfall."

"Yes, even with the sleigh, it is tedious work for the horses to find the least troublesome areas to move through."

My mind was in a daze. As Charles and Joshua continued to talk quietly about the results of the test, I was thinking about the future. What if the malignancy spread? How would I handle the farm alone? I could barely get the livestock taken care of in an emergency!

The next few days moved by as if in slow motion. I was consumed with dread and fear. All the peaceful feelings of a few days earlier were replaced with questions that had no answers. How could God allow this to happen? Joshua was one of the kindest, most helpful elders in the meeting. He was needed by so many! God could not take him now when the work was far from complete! Perhaps He was just testing us! Like He tested Abraham when he asked him to sacrifice his only son. God had provided a ram just as Abraham was about to plunge the knife. Yes! That must be the answer! God was testing Joshua and me to see how strong our faith was!

I would not fail the test! I would put my entire trust in God!

———

It was only a few days before my faith would again be severely tested. When I answered a knock on the door, I was shocked to see my brother-in-law, Daniel. From the look on his face, I knew the news was not good.

"Daniel! Come in! Thee looks frozen! How long has thee been riding!"

"For the past three days!" he sobbed. "I could not stay there! I had to try and get to thee!"

"Thee has been riding for three days straight?" I asked incredulously.

"Of course, I spent the nights at Friends' homes along the way. But most of the time I was wading snow drifts with my horse. I thought I would never get here!"

Grasping his shoulders, I helped him remove his now nearly solid wraps. "Come and sit down and let me get thee a hot cup of coffee. Then thee can tell us what has happened."

Reluctantly, Daniel did as I asked, moving in a daze.

Rising from the bed and moving slowly to the table, Joshua began to wrap Daniel in a quilt to quiet his chilling body. When the coffee and warm blanket began to revive him, I asked the question I was not sure I wanted to know the answer to.

"Is it Abigail? Has something happened to her?"

"Abigail is fine, but the baby is dead!" he burst out.

He then began to sob uncontrollably as we waited for him to tell us his story of sorrow. Never could we have imagined just one short year ago how severely our faith would be tested in this winter of despair!

16

Ministering

D aniel finally managed to get warmed, at least in body. The tragedy which had besought him and his wife would not be so easily overcome.

"Can thee talk about what happened?" I asked gently when it seemed he was ready to share his ordeal with us. "Is Abigail all right? Thee did not leave her alone, I pray!"

"No, I did not leave her alone. One of the neighbor ladies was kind enough to stay with her while I traveled to see thee. As for being all right, I do not know for certain that she will ever be the same!" Daniel said, anguish evident in his voice. "She wanted this child more than she wanted anything in life!"

"Tell us what happened," Joshua encouraged.

"I knew Abigail should have been staying in bed," Daniel began. "The doctor had told us there might be a problem when I took her to see him after she had been experiencing some pain. He said she should not do anything strenuous, and it would be best if she stayed down as much as possible. But thee knows Abigail!

"We had a shipment arrive on the railroad just before this last snowstorm. I was a mile or so from home cutting more wood in anticipation of the blizzard when they arrived. Abigail was afraid to send one of the passengers to get me, as she did not want them to risk being sighted. For some reason she decided to take them to the cave herself, even though some of the path was through deep snow!

"Why did she have to do that?" he asked in anguish. "Why could she not have waited for me?!"

"What other choices did she have?" Joshua asked kindly.

"I wish she had just left them in the cabin until I got there!"

"Was it safe for the passengers there?"

"No, that was the problem. Two slave catchers had just been at our cabin a few hours before, searching every square inch of the building. Abigail was afraid for the lives of the passengers, and she felt she had to take them to safety."

"What would thee have done if thee had been in her place?" I asked quietly.

"I do not know for certain, but if I had been carrying a child—a child that might not survive if I did not take care of my own body—I would have tried to find another solution!"

"Does thee not think Abigail tried to think of another possibility? Did thee not say she considered sending one of the slaves to get thee?"

"Yes, I suppose thee is right."

"And is it not possible that Abigail did what she thought she had to do to save the lives of the passengers who had come to her for help?" Joshua patiently asked.

"But she lost the baby!" he exclaimed, once again near tears.

"Yes, but thee said she was spared, did thee not?"

"Yes, and I am grateful for that. It was fortunate that one of the women in the shipment was a midwife and was willing to risk her own safety to help when Abigail went into labor."

"Did the doctor know why the baby did not survive?"

"When he was finally able to make it to the cabin, several days had passed. The only thing he could say for certain was that the baby probably did not survive because it was too soon for it to be born and its lungs were not fully developed."

"How does Abigail feel about the loss?"

"She does not say anything at all. In fact, when I try to talk with her about it, she quickly changes the subject! I could not stand to be in the cabin another day, knowing that our baby might be alive if I had been more careful!"

"Daniel!" Joshua said sternly. "That is nonsense! Thee was working to prepare for a blizzard! Thee was being careful to meet the needs of thy wife and unborn child! There is no reason thee should feel responsible for this tragedy!"

"Then who is responsible?" he demanded. "I have tried to be obedient to the Light within. I have risked my life to save the lives of my fellow men. What have I received in return? The loss of my first-born. My first son!"

"I am so sorry!" I said, moving to his side to try and comfort him. "I know thee is feeling the loss right now, and it is good for thee to grieve. Only time is going to heal this wound...and prayer. Thee must believe God is still in control of thy life and the life of thy wife."

Even as the words left my mouth I wondered if I meant them. It was easy to tell someone else to trust in God and believe in His promises. When it came to one's own life, however, sometimes doubt still remained.

"I am sorry to have fallen apart like that," Daniel finally said when he had regained control of his emotions.

"I knew thee would want to know, Rebecca, and I knew thee and Joshua would help me see the good in the situation. Just being able to talk about it with thee has begun to lift the burden."

"I am so glad thee was able to make it here! I cannot imagine how thee managed to travel from Springdale through the drifted snow and cold!" I said admiringly.

"The main reason I came was to see if thee would travel back with me to spend some time with thy sister. She will not talk to me, but I believe she might share her feelings with thee, Rebecca. Thee has always been close to her."

I quickly looked at Joshua. We had not told anyone of the news of his malignant growth, and I did not want to leave him in case he developed more tumors.

Finally, Joshua decided Daniel should be told about his condition before any decisions were made about my traveling north.

"I am so sorry to hear that, Joshua," he said sadly after hearing of the test results. "It seems like this family is cursed. Two disasters in two months!"

"Just because the tests were positive does not mean Joshua will not recover completely!" I added quickly. "In fact, we are trusting God to continue the healing."

"I suppose we should look at the positive side," Daniel agreed. After inquiring about Joshua's present health, he again asked if it would be possible for me to return with him.

"I could not leave Joshua right now!" I said emphatically. "I need to take care of him and make sure he stays in good health!"

"Rebecca! Thee knows I am getting stronger by the day. I can cook for myself and even wash my clothes if I need to. I think thee should go and spend some time with thy sister. She needs thee much more than I do right now. Thee can spend a few weeks with her and when thee returns, I should be nearly mended and ready to resume some of the work around the farm. By then perhaps much of the snow will have melted and I can begin to repair fences, or get the equipment ready for spring planting. Thee knows Jacob will continue to tend the livestock, so there is really no reason for thee not to return with Daniel!"

"But I do not think I could ride Samson through the drifts," I argued. "He is too old for such strenuous work!"

"I have already thought of that!" Joshua continued. "Daniel can ride to the Johnsons and see if he might borrow their sleigh to transport thee to Springdale. Then he could return the sleigh whenever they needed it, perhaps even keeping it until the time comes for thee to return."

"I do not think we should impose on Luke's good nature that way!" I protested. "How would he get his family to meeting? Thee knows they usually all ride together in that old sleigh of his!"

"Luke only lives a quarter mile from the meeting house, Rebecca. If he needed to, he could take the children one or two at a time on horseback until they were all transported there."

"But I have responsibilities here...my patients...."

"Rebecca, thee knows thy workload has not been heavy this winter," Joshua said quietly. "Folks are staying inside more, and there is not the demand right now that there will be when spring arrives. I am certain Charles will be able to cover for thee."

When it became obvious that each of my arguments was going to be successfully countered, I resigned myself to visiting Abigail. It was not that I did not want to see her; but what would I say to a woman who just lost her first child while trying to do a good deed for others? And what if Joshua became ill while I was away?

As if reading my mind, Joshua sought to reassure me. "I will send for thee if my health should take a turn for the worse. Dr. Jones has said he would continue to check on me from time to time, so there is no need for thee to worry!"

"Good!" Daniel joined in. "I am feeling so much better than I was just a few hours ago when I thought my world was coming to an end! If thee will excuse me, I will check on my poor horse that I so quickly abandoned and see if he is able to travel to the Johnsons. I believe I remember where their cabin is."

Once his mind was settled, he quickly put on his now

dry clothes that I had hung in front of the fire when he first arrived. When he was gone, I began preparing for the journey, still voicing my disapproval to Joshua.

"Thy sister needs thee much more than I. Go and be a blessing to her," he finished as he made his way to the bed for a much deserved rest.

"Thee will make certain and get word to me if thy condition changes?"

"Yes, of course. Have a good trip, and please convey my sympathy to thy sister."

"Very well," I said, beginning to feel somewhat better about my journey.

———————

We made the trip to Springdale in much less time than I had anticipated. Perhaps the journey went quickly because of the tales of the Underground Railroad that Daniel provided me.

"Has thee ever heard of John Brown?" he asked after we had both reaffirmed our disgust with the institution of slavery.

"No, I do not believe I have. Is he a Friend?"

"No," Daniel laughed, "though some Friends would like to claim him! John Brown is a noted Abolitionist who has spent nearly twenty years trying to educate poor black children. This past year he followed five of his sons to the Midwest to fight against a group of marauding pro-slavery terrorists from Missouri who had killed a number of abolitionists in Lawrence."

"That is in the Kansas Territory, is it not?" I asked, trying to remember my geography.

"Yes, toward the eastern border. Many believe there will be much bloodshed from Brown and his sons to retaliate for these murders.

"This is all very interesting, Daniel, but what affect does it have on thee and thy operation?"

"Actually, none at the moment. My fear is that these Abolitionists will negate all the good that has been done to try and stop slavery. Killing others will not help their cause!"

"As a Friend, does thee support this man?" I asked, curious to know his opinion.

"I support his abhorrence of the institution of slavery, but I certainly can not condone the use of violence to oppose it! And to answer thy earlier question, the reason I am speaking of this to thee is because there are some Friends in Springdale who believe in this man and his approach. There is even talk of having him come here to begin preparation for a big raid sometime in the next year or two.

"I am worried, Rebecca. I believe some of the members of Springdale Friends will see John Brown's plan as a great cause to support!"

"But if he is trying to put an end to the institution of slavery, why does thee fear Friends becoming involved?"

"Thee knows the scripture, Rebecca. Christ was quite emphatic about not using violence to solve social ills. In fact, he said we were to turn the other cheek when our enemy does evil to us."

"Yes, but if thee will remember, he also became angry with the money-changers in the temple."

"I do not believe that is the same. All his teachings were of peace and serving others, not killing them! I am afraid we are traveling down the wrong road if we become allies with this man.

"And yet, I can understand his hatred of slavery. Even more so now that I have been personally involved with helping people to freedom."

"How many Friends does thee think will join with this John Brown?"

"I am hoping there will be many strong voices in meeting to speak against the use of violence. I believe if we are faithful to the Light of God, He will reveal his will to us. My worst fear is that my cousin George will join Brown's cause if he does come to Springdale."

"I hope George will listen to thee and the others who might speak against the methods of this man. In the meantime, I want thee to know how much I admire thee and Abigail for the part thee are playing in helping the Negroes escape to freedom. I believe it takes a great deal of bravery to do what thee is doing!"

"If a person believes in a cause, Rebecca, I think he must act on that cause. Does thee remember what James said in chapter two, verse seventeen of his epistle? He said, 'Even so faith, if it hath not works, is dead, being alone.' I believe our faith in God compels us to action, and I simply could not sit in meeting week after week worshiping God yet allowing an evil institution like slavery to continue!"

Having spoken his mind, Daniel was consumed by his own thoughts the remainder of the trip, as I was with mine. I was glad I had come, knowing my ministry at this time was to my sister, not home hovering over Joshua! This was not the first time I had discovered new truths when I escaped from the four walls of our cabin!

Abigail was glad to see us when we arrived, not realizing Daniel had intended to bring me back with him.

"I am so sorry!" were my first words to this special sister.

"I thank thee, Rebecca. I am feeling much better now. It has been good for me to spend time with Vera, our neighbor across the creek. She helped me realize how fortunate I was to still be in good health and have a husband who loves me like Daniel."

"Where is Vera?" Daniel interrupted.

"I sent her home, dear. She had been away from her family for too long as it was. I knew I would be fine until thee returned. I also thought we might receive new passengers, and I did not know how I would explain them to her!"

"Did anyone arrive?" he asked tensely.

"No, I suppose the deep snow and tracks make it too dangerous to travel."

"I am glad thee did not have to handle it alone. I doubt we will have any more passengers until the snow melts; in fact, that is one of the reasons I felt comfortable leaving thee to cut wood the day..." he paused, not wanting to re-open the wound.

"The day we lost our son," she finished quietly. "It was not meant to be, Daniel. God may bless us with another child some day, and in the meantime we will have to think of these black children who sometimes come our way as our own."

"I am so glad to hear thee say that," Daniel exclaimed as he squeezed her hand warmly. "I was so worried about thee! I should never have left thee the way I did! I simply did not know what else to do!"

"We will go on from here, dear. We have our ministry and we will do what we can to fight the evil curse of slavery! Did thee tell Rebecca about John Brown?"

"Yes, we talked about his possible journey here to pre-pare for battle."

"I am afraid it is more than just talk! Word is that he will definitely be arriving here sometime within the next year to train for the mission, and thy cousin George is eager to join!"

"I was afraid of that! I will try to see him as soon as possible. Perhaps he will reconsider before the time comes."

"I hope so, Nothing good can come from violence, Daniel, thee knows that!"

"Yes, I know that, but there is a certain attraction to a cause that feels free to circumvent the law for its own pur-poses!"

"I am worried about this country, Daniel," Abigail con-tinued. "Nothing good can come of this evil. Nothing good at all!"

17

Love Endures

I enjoyed my visit with Abigail, but after the third week, I was anxious to return home. There was really nothing for me to do in their small cabin; I did help Abigail with a few sewing projects, one of which was to finish stitching a small quilt she had started before losing the baby.

It was a relief to feel no overwhelming grief when doing the handwork. I knew that just a year ago I would not have been able to stitch the quilt. God had certainly answered my prayers!

I also was called upon to help deliver a baby for one of the members of Springdale Meeting. I had been reluctant to go, but Daniel assured me the family had heard all about my abilities and wanted me to come. Fortunately, there were no complications and both mother and child were doing well. I was extremely pleased when they gave her the middle name of Rebecca!

I was careful not to speak of the birth with Abigail, though she did ask about the delivery and the health of both mother and child. Even though she was putting forth a brave front, I knew she still grieved for the child she had lost.

At the end of the fourth week, I persuaded Daniel to take me home. As Joshua had predicted, Luke had been happy to lend us his sleigh for as long as we needed it. He said there were others in the community who would be glad to give him the use of a sleigh if the family needed to travel further than the meeting house.

As I prepared to leave, both Daniel and Abigail thanked me over and over for coming to minister to them. I felt a bit embarrassed; after all, they were part of my family. I invited them to visit as soon as the crops were planted, and they both assured me they would do so.

"I am anxious to talk to Joshua again," Daniel said. "I certainly hope he is still feeling well."

"Of course he is!" Abigail said firmly. "Everyone in Pleasant Plain Quarterly Meeting, as well as those in the Springdale Quarter, have been praying for his continued recovery. Thee knows the power of prayer!"

"Abigail is right, Rebecca," Daniel agreed. "Thee and Joshua have many friends in this part of the state!"

It was an affirmation to my faith, and I left their home feeling better than I had in a long time.

———————

"Rebecca! I am so glad to see thee!" Joshua greeted me as I entered the cabin. He was smiling, and I felt a joy well up inside as I gave him a big hug.

"Is thee all right?" I asked anxiously.

"I am doing well," he said simply.

"Thee is sure there has been no new tumor?"

"As I said, I feel well. I have even begun to do a few chores—with Jacob's assistance, of course."

"Is thee certain thee will not reinjure thy wound?"

Joshua's laugh, though strong, seemed a bit strained. "Rebecca, my dear, the surgery was nearly five months ago!

Those stitches have healed long ago, and I hardly feel any pain when moving around. Of course, I will take it easy for awhile. That is why I have only been going out when Jacob is here. He is nearly as bad as thee, though. He refuses to let me do anything but the simplest tasks."

"Good for him. Thee does not always use the best judgment when it comes to knowing thy limits!"

Just then Jacob arrived to do the chores. He and Daniel began to visit about the Railroad, and Jacob asked him about John Brown. News in Salem was that Brown was looking for recruits and that he would be in Springdale sometime this fall.

"Thee does not believe in Brown's methods, does thee?" Jacob inquired. "It is hard for me to justify taking the lives of men to fight slavery."

"That is exactly my opinion!" Daniel heartily agreed. "No, I do not agree with his methods. But apparently there are some who do."

"Jacob has been speaking to me about this subject," Joshua broke in, "but I did not know enough of the circumstances to form an opinion. Could thee tell me a bit more about this man?"

Just as he had done with me on our ride to Springdale, Daniel told Joshua everything he knew about John Brown.

"It is a pity that Friends have become associated with this man and his operation," Joshua said sadly when Daniel had finished the story.

"And the saddest part of all is that my cousin George is planning to join with Brown. First and foremost I am worried about his safety. When one party feels free to use deadly weapons, those of the other side feel the same freedom. It scares me, Joshua!"

"We will keep thee and thy cousin in our prayers, Daniel. Perhaps he will see the error of Brown's thinking before becoming too deeply involved."

"I thank thee, Joshua. Now I must be on my way. I

need to return the sleigh to the Johnsons and get as far north as possible before dark."

"Thee just wants to get back to Abby," Jacob teased.

"Thee had best hold thy tongue, young man," Daniel shot back. "I hear thee has been traveling to Salem quite often these days. And it is not just to get supplies!"

Jacob laughed, clearly comfortable with his growing closeness to Freda. "Thee never knows, Daniel. The next time thee visits our part of the state it just might be for a wedding!"

"Jacob!" I exclaimed. "When did thee decide to get married?"

"Well, we have not officially become engaged. Freda is planning to attend school in Iowa City this fall, and I would like to pass meeting before she leaves. That way we can set a date and make plans during the coming year."

"What does she plan to study at Iowa University?" I asked curiously.

"She is planning on a one-year study of nursing. Ever since Dr. Jones has been attending Salem Friends he has encouraged her to consider becoming a nurse. She has been helping in his office these past few weeks and has grown to love working with the patients who come to see him."

"Charles did not mention Freda was working for him," I said slowly, a strange feeling overcoming me.

"When was the last time thee talked to him, Rebecca? Thee has been gone for a month."

"I have not spoken with him since the day he came with thee in the sleigh. I suppose it has been a while."

Why was I feeling this way? For some reason the thought of Freda working daily with Charles was distressing to me. As ridiculous as it seemed, I felt annoyed to know someone else was sharing his practice—someone besides me!

Trying to put my feelings aside, I congratulated my brother. "I am really happy for thee, Jacob. Thee deserves a good wife, and Freda seems to love thee a great deal."

This time I sensed Jacob's embarrassment, but I knew he felt the same way.

"Tell me more about her working with Charles," I found myself saying.

"There is nothing else to tell, Rebecca. She simply helps him with the patients if he needs her, and does some of his bookkeeping as well. He feels fortunate to have her. Oh...and did I tell thee he became a member of Salem Friends several weeks ago?"

"No," I said simply, turning to busy myself with unpacking.

What else had been going on in his life that I did not know about? What had happened to our closeness? We used to share our lives with each other, I thought sadly, and now I do not know anything that is important to him.

The news of Charles continued to disturb me long after Daniel and Jacob left. Finally, Joshua quit asking me questions about my visit, probably tired of one-syllable answers!

"What is troubling thee, Rebecca?" he finally asked. "Is thee worried about Abigail and how she will manage without thee?"

"No, I suppose I am just weary from the long trip home. I think I will lie down and rest awhile."

"I am sorry thee has not had a chance to visit with Charles lately. Perhaps thee should consider making a trip to Salem tomorrow to catch up on the news. The snow was nearly gone when thee came home, was it not?"

"Yes it was, and there would be no trouble traveling. The ground is still frozen and the snow is packed. We made good time coming from Springdale." I paused, trying to decide whether or not to share my thoughts with Joshua.

"Perhaps I will visit Charles tomorrow," I finally said, deciding to work through my feelings on my own. "It would be good to see if he has received any more medical journals. And I never did get to speak with him about his conference in St. Louis."

More than anything, I simply wanted to see and talk to this man I respected—and cared about, I realized.

———————————

My visit with Charles was wonderful. He asked me about my sister and what I had done while away. I told him about the delivery I had assisted in, and reassured him that Abigail was doing well, both physically and emotionally.

"So tell me, how does thee like thy new assistant?" I asked, trying not to show the anxiety I felt.

"Oh, Freda? She is a godsend, Rebecca. She is so willing to learn, and she has a great love for the patients who come into the office. I presume Jacob told thee of his desire to pass meetings before she leaves for school this fall?"

"Yes, he said he was hopeful. How does thee feel about losing her?"

"Well, that I will regret, but Jacob is a fine young man and they will have a good marriage. Don't you think so?" he asked, suddenly curious about my questions.

"Oh yes!" I said quickly. "I think they will easily pass both meetings now that her father feels more kindly toward Jacob."

"His concerns were not so much with Jacob as they were with Freda continuing her schooling. He was most pleased when she told him of her plans to attend Iowa University.

"How do you feel about the marriage?" he asked quietly. "Do you have any doubts?"

"No," I said, trying to sound reassuring. "I am happy they have each other."

"And Joshua?" he asked, changing the subject. "Is he still feeling healthy?"

"If thee means to ask if there have been any new tumors, the answer is no. He assures me he is feeling fine.

Knowing Joshua, however, it would not surprise me if he kept any changes to himself!"

"If he did so, he would only be trying to protect you, wouldn't he?"

"I do not need to be protected!" I nearly shouted. "Why do you men think we women are all weak-kneed and fragile? Why must you keep things from us that you believe we can not handle?!"

Charles laughed out loud and quickly sought to amend his previous statement.

"I'm sorry, Rebecca. I should never have said Joshua might be trying to protect you. You are one of the strongest women I know, and that is why I like you so well—and why I've missed you so much this winter!"

His words were like a cool drink on a warm day. So refreshing! Charles still cared about me, and he had missed me while I had been gone.

"I am sorry for my outburst!" I laughed, suddenly feeling light-hearted again. "My outspoken ways have gotten me in trouble more than once in my life!"

"Never be ashamed of speaking your feelings, my dear. Too many people suffer from all sorts of maladies because they keep their feelings buried deep inside them."

"And thee?" I asked quietly. "Has thee suffered from thy past which thee has kept hidden all these years?"

"Now you are asking personal questions!" he said with a smile. "Actually, I have felt much better about my past since the afternoon I shared with you the story of how I lost my wife and child. It was a sort of healing, I suppose, but I have come to the place where I can now thank God for the time I had with Julia."

"That reminds me—Jacob tells me thee has become a member of the Salem Meeting. I am very pleased!"

"It was a decision that took some careful consideration, but eventually I felt the need to belong to a group of people who viewed the world in ways similar to my beliefs. I still find it hard to get to meeting every week, but when I do attend I can feel the Spirit moving in the midst, and I feel blessed."

Charles and I continued to visit until he was summoned to care for one of his elderly patients who was near death.

"I am certainly glad you decided to come for a visit today," he said warmly as I rose to leave. He helped me with my wraps and then suddenly gave me a quick hug. "Don't stay away so long the next time!" And with that he was out the door.

I stood stunned for a moment. Charles had never so much as shaken my hand in the past. What was the meaning of the hug?

Rebecca, thee is a fool! I chided myself. He gave thee a hug because he was glad to see thee—an old and dear friend. Go home to thy husband and forget about this man.

It was easy to talk to myself, but not so easy to stop the thoughts that continued to dance in my mind the rest of the day.

"How was thy visit with Charles?" Joshua inquired as soon as I walked through the door.

"We had a good visit. He is grateful to have Freda working for him, and he did join the Salem Meeting. Which he is enjoying, I might add."

"That is all?" he asked when I did not say more. "Thee was gone for five hours! Surely thee talked about more than that!"

"It takes an hour each way to travel there, thee must remember, and we were interrupted several times while trying to catch up on news," I finished, unwilling to discuss it further.

"It must have been a good visit," Joshua said warily. "I have not seen thee smile so much in many months!"

Knowing I must quickly end any suspicions he might have, I reassured him that we spoke mostly of patients and that my isolation this winter had been difficult. I told him how happy I was just to be able to travel once again and resume my visits with Charles.

"I am happy thee feels so positive about thy work—and this man. I have known for a long time that thee felt especially close to him, even when thee could not visit as often as thee would have liked. I should be sad, but in the end it may be for the best."

"What does thee mean?" I asked, suddenly alarmed at his tone of voice.

"I did not want to tell thee this, Rebecca. In fact, I had thought perhaps it would be best if I spared thee. The more I thought about it, however, the more I realized I was not being honest by trying to protect thee."

My face turned white, knowing with strange certainty what his next words would be.

"The truth is, while thee was gone I discovered a growth under my arm, and two days ago another appeared close to the place where Charles removed the first. It looks like God has chosen to answer our prayers in a different way than we had hoped."

"But thee said thee felt fine when I asked about thy health! Thee said there had been no new tumors!"

"I am sorry, Rebecca. But I did not say there were no new growths; I simply said I felt fine. And I do."

"Thee should have sent word to me!" I cried. "Thee promised!"

"As I said, I have felt well, and the growths did not appear until a few days ago. There would have been no time to get a message to thee."

"Why?... Why? Why? Why?" I cried out, to God as much as to Joshua. "I was certain He would heal thee! There were so many Friends praying for thee. Thee has been such an important part of the East Grove Meeting. How can God take thee away from us? How can he take thee away from me?!" I asked tearfully, trying to be strong for this man I loved.

"I do not have answers, Rebecca. But believe me when I say it is for the best. God always knows what is best if we trust Him."

"How can it be for the best?" I demanded.

"Time will tell, and I believe Paul speaks truth in Romans 8:28 when he says, 'And we know that all things work together for good to them that love God, to them who are called according to his purpose.'"

"What good can come of this? What earthly good can come from someone being taken from their loved ones?" I asked myself. What good at all?

18

My Grace Is Sufficient
for Thee

In the days that followed Joshua's disclosure of the new growths, we spent a great deal of time discussing how we would handle his certain death within a matter of weeks.

The first decision I made was to quit treating patients until Joshua...I did not even like to think of what I knew was to come!

"Thee will do no such thing!" he declared. "Thy work is important to the people of this community. I still feel quite well and I intend to continue living my life in the most normal way possible."

"But what will thee say to the others? Will thee tell them of thy illness?"

"I want both our families to know. My parents will be supportive, as will yours. I have not decided whether I will speak to Friends at meeting. I do not want them to pity me, yet I feel a need to be honest. I would appreciate thy prayers on the matter."

"In other words, thee intends for our lives to continue as always—at least for as long as possible."

"Will thee be able to do that?" he asked gently.

"Joshua, thee is the one that must live with the possibilities of what may occur in the future. I can certainly go about my business, but it will be extremely difficult for me to act as if nothing has changed!"

"I realize the pain thee must feel, and I wish there was something I could do to smooth the way for thee."

Just like Joshua...always thinking of another rather than himself. I determined then and there to be the strong partner, to do my best to hide the grief that rose up within me at the thought of losing him.

When we traveled to Salem to tell Charles the news, it was almost as though a member of his own family had been stricken.

"This is one of the times I hate being a doctor!" he said, slamming his fist onto the examining table. "We have no idea where these tumors originate, and no idea how to treat them. We could try and remove the new growths, but the pain and suffering of the surgeries would not be worth the few weeks you might gain.

"Please tell me what I might do to help you through this time. I feel so responsible for giving you false hope!"

"Please do not feel apologetic," Joshua said quickly. "If thee had told me I was probably going to die, I would not have enjoyed the last few months nearly as much as I have."

"Thee was only giving thy opinion, anyway," I joined in, "and thee was careful to tell us thee could not be certain about the tumor."

I could tell Charles was not taking the news well, his whole demeanor having changed. He was usually quite stoic, never letting his patients guess his true feelings. In some ways it was a relief. I had worried about his inability to show his emotions; there always seemed to be so much buried beneath the surface. Perhaps he was willing to be vulnerable again; more open to allowing his emotions the freedom to be expressed.

"I was surprised by Charles' reaction to my news," Joshua said on our way home that day. "He has never been one to show how he felt—at least not to his patients."

"Thee is so right. If nothing else, thy disease has helped one man come to terms with the pain in his past."

Joshua looked at me strangely, but did not inquire further when I did not elaborate.

"That is what we need to do, Rebecca. We need to continually look for the good in the midst of our difficulties. I have asked God to use my life as a blessing to others these last days, and perhaps we have just received the first blessing."

———————

Joshua continued to look for the positive in his life. Perhaps one of the most meaningful meetings ever held at East Grove Friends occurred the morning he asked for an open meeting.

As was common with the Society of Friends, the men met for worship on one side of the meeting house and the women on the other. There was a partition dividing the two, with a moveable shutter in middle that was opened when business needed to be conducted between sides.

On this particular morning, we sat in the silence for quite some time, possibly an hour or more. My heart was heavy as I could not seem to center down, thoughts of the future crowding out thoughts of worship. The possibility of losing Joshua was just now beginning to seem real as his suffering from the tumors had increased more recently.

When Joshua asked to speak to both meetings, the shutter was opened for all to hear his words.

"Friends," he began, "I have a message from the Holy Spirit for you today. This message has been laid on my heart like a burning coal, and I must tell it to you."

He paused, as if wanting to make sure the message was exactly what the Spirit had given him.

"The Spirit within me is calling us to be a holy people. We have come to this land to spread the news that Jesus Christ died for the sins of mankind, and that personal salvation is available for all. We have begun a good work, but I fear we are becoming complacent.

"When was the last time you spoke to your unsaved neighbor? When was the last time you knelt with a friend and prayed with them for healing? Healing of their soul as well as their body?

"And what of your thoughts? The apostle Paul said we were to think on whatsoever was pure, and whatsoever was lovely, and whatsoever was holy. Have you been thinking about furthering the kingdom of God, or have your lives become consumed with chores and planting and harvesting?

"Yes, we all wear our simple clothing, and speak with our thees and thous, but are we continuing the work we were sent to do? Has the missionary zeal faded?

"Oh, my Friends....I fear for the well-being of this meeting. Our membership has declined. It is true, some left because they could not tolerate the slave catchers that frequent our cities and farms; some have left for greed—they desired more and better land which the West promised; and some have left because Satan has lured them away from the truth. He has convinced them that it will make no difference if they follow the Light within, that the only life we will have is here on earth so we had best enjoy it while we can.

"Well, dear Friends, I am here to tell you today that life is indeed short. In fact, for me life is but a few days or weeks. The doctor has told me there is no cure for the tumors that have beset my body. But I am not sad; on the contrary, I am joyful! I am excited! I am going to see my risen Saviour soon.

"Of course I am sorrowful for what I must leave behind. My dear wife Rebecca will need your support in the days to come. She has given me everything a woman could give a man—and more. I have loved her since I was twelve years old, and I will love her for eternity.

"And my good friends and neighbors...I will miss each of you. But I do not want you to grieve for my passing into the next life. Once again the apostle Paul speaks to us when he admits he had a thorn in the flesh. Three times, he said, he prayed to God for deliverance, and three times God said, 'My grace is sufficient for thee.'

"Those words have been a great comfort for me these past few weeks. For I know that the grace of our God is indeed sufficient for me, just as it is sufficient for you, my friends. Today I am asking you to make a fresh commitment to God the Father, Jesus His Son, and the Holy Spirit. I am asking you to once again seek God's face and experience the power of His Holy Spirit within you.

"The time is short, my friends. Jesus may return at any hour. I would ask you this day to consider your walk with Him. Pray for forgiveness of your sins and turn once again to the path of righteouness. God is calling you today. Answer the call; follow his bidding; be the servant he is calling you to be!"

When Joshua once again pulled the divider, the sorrow of the women around me could be heard. I was certain the same was true on the men's side. I felt a calm reassurance that all would be well, that God would take care of me. I also knew that Joshua had been a messenger of the Holy Spirit, and that lives would be changed because he had been willing to speak the message he had been given.

From the time he shared what the Spirit laid on his heart until his passing two weeks later, the outpouring of love from the community was astounding. Nearly everyone came, offering to help in any way possible. Perhaps the most blessed thing to happen was when several members who had fallen away came to tell us how Joshua's message had caused them to renew their commitment to the Lord.

I will never forget our final conversation. I knew Joshua's hours were numbered; the pain was intense and several more tumors had appeared. As I was rubbing his back to ease the pain, once again he told me of the gift of love God had given him for me.

"I feel so blessed to have lived with thee these years," I returned, "even though I have not always been the loving wife thee deserved. Thee has taught me what it means to be unselfish by thy example to our friends in the community and at meeting. I must tell thee, Joshua, I resented thee for many years because I felt thee was concerned about everyone else but me. It was not until I began to treat others that I experienced the joy of service."

"Jesus himself said that he who is the least on earth will be the greatest in heaven, and that has always been my goal: to be a servant for the Lord.

"I would like for thee to read a passage from the Word to me if thee would. It helps take my mind off of...other things."

Even in the midst of his pain he sought to be humble. Thumbing through the familiar scriptures, I chose one of our favorites, I Corinthians thirteen. When I finished, Joshua asked me to reread the middle portion.

"'Charity suffereth long, and is kind; charity envieth not; charity vaunteth not itself, is not puffed up. Doth not behave itself unseemly, seeketh not her own, is not easily provoked, thinketh no evil; Rejoiceth not in iniquity, but rejoiceth in the truth; Beareth all things, believeth all things, hopeth all things, endureth all things' Thy life has been fulfilled in these verses, Joshua. I am so proud of the example thee has given for others—including me—to follow!"

"I only have one regret, however. And that is that I could not produce a child for thee. I know how very much thee wanted a family."

"It was for the best, Joshua. God had a plan for my life, but I wanted my own way. How would I have managed a child without thee? It is much better for me to be alone, with my friends and my practice. Once I gave the matter over to God, I was at peace. So thee should be as well."

"Thee is so young, Rebecca, I pray thee will remarry when God chooses to give thee another husband."

"I will never remarry, Joshua, how can thee even think of such a thing at a time like this? I have grown to love thee deeply, and I will carry that love with me always. I have no fear of the future. God will provide if I keep my trust in Him."

"It is not always an easy life for a widow, Rebecca. Just keep thy heart open. I have a feeling there is someone who would marry thee right now if thee wished."

"Maybe someone, somewhere, but right now I only want to think of thee. Please...can we speak of something else?"

"I will never mention this again, Rebecca, but Charles Jones loves thee in a special way. I can see it in his admiring eyes when he looks at thee. And some day if thee is honest with thyself thee will also admit that Charles has a special place in thy heart."

"As I said, Joshua, I do not intend to remarry. End of subject. Now, I think thee should rest. Thee has been speaking more now than thee should have."

I quickly left his side and sat in front of the window, the May breeze cooling my brow and clearing my mind. I could not understand why Joshua had thought I might be interested in Charles. I admired and respected him, but that was all. How could he doubt my love for him now?

Where Joshua had gotten the strength for our conversation that night I would never know, but it must have been divine for he passed on while he slept, on to a better life with his Saviour.

The funeral was conducted in the manner of Friends; a solemn occasion where each present was expected to reflect on the shortness of life and whether or not they themselves were prepared for eternity. Many members rose to speak of the impact this one man had had on them. Several shared the way their lives had been changed after Joshua spoke in meeting that last time.

I did not purchase a gravestone as many Friends were now doing, but rather had a simple marker placed over the grave. Joshua had made it clear that he considered stones to be inconsistent with his belief in simplicity. Luke Johnson had lovingly made a plain coffin for his good friend, and on the lid inscribed both our names to be joined forever.

I remained surprisingly at peace throughout the ordeal, my tears having been shed weeks before. I knew Joshua was happy to be with the Lord, and I would be happy for him. My life would never be the same, but it had been enriched by this man God had given me to love. The love of this Friend, Joshua Frazier, would remain with me forever.

19

New Beginnings

The days and months following Joshua's passing were much harder to endure than I had anticipated. It was one thing to believe God was in control of the situation, quite another to feel good about it.

Joshua's presence was everywhere I turned those first days: at the livestock paddock, in the calf shed, at the wood pile, sitting at the kitchen table over a steaming cup of coffee, and worst of all, in bed at night. It was there I felt the most alone. There was no comforting snore, no arm around my waist, no one to share confidences with.

Friends were good to visit, though often I sensed they did not know what to say and were uncomfortable being in the cabin. I longed to tell them that their presence alone meant more than any words they could say, but I did not want to offend them.

Betty came as often as she could, but our friendship had been strained by the demands of her family and my frequent journeys to treat patients. And even my practice was suffering; it was as if friends and neighbors felt I would not be able to handle any medical duties because of Joshua's death.

I wanted to shout: It was Joshua who was sick, not "I!" But again, I did not want people to feel ill at ease.

And so I sat day after day, with nothing to do but think about Joshua's absence and become even more lonely. I did not feel like traveling to Salem to visit Charles, and he had only been to the cabin once since Joshua's passing. I knew he was busy—probably because he had to treat a number of my former patients! There was also the remembrance of Joshua's final words to me concerning Charles. I was not certain how I felt about him now that I was a widow, and I certainly did not want to deal with any new emotions just yet.

I continued to go to meeting, of course, though the Spirit seemed far away. I left as quickly as possible when the worship service was finished, trying to avoid well- meaning Friends whose questions were too much for me to deal with.

Jacob was my one ray of sunshine. He had taken over the farm work and always stopped in for a visit, even if only for a few moments. He and Freda had passed both the Salem and East Grove Meetings and were making plans for a September wedding following Freda's graduation. His happiness was contagious, and my spirits were often lifted by the time he rose to leave.

I remembered how he had struggled with school after having a difficult teacher at an early age, and I marveled at the fine young man he had become. In many ways he reminded me of Joshua, and I told him so one day as we sat discussing current business at East Grove Friends.

"I am really proud of thee, Jacob," I had told him. "Thee has become such an important member of our meeting. In fact, thee has nearly taken the place Joshua used to hold: chief helper to those in need!"

"I could never take Joshua's, place, Rebecca. I don't think thee ever really knew just how much he did for others. I'm surprised he ever had time to do his own work! I have tried to respond to people's needs, but I am too busy with both the farms to be the kind of servant Joshua was. Thee should know, though, that his example was what gave me the desire to help others. I have always been overly concerned with my own problems, and Joshua helped me see what a blessing it is to give assistance to those in need."

"Yes, he certainly thought of others before himself," I agreed.

The more we talked that day, the more an idea began to grow in my mind.

"Jacob," I inquired, "where will thee and Freda live after thee are married?"

"That is a good question. Freda would like to live where we can be close to a town, but I need to be near the livestock and farm land. I suppose we will ask Friends to help us raise a cabin; I have been trying to get a few logs cut, but it seems like the days are either too short or too cold to accomplish much. In a few weeks it will be planting season, and my wood cutting will come to a halt.

"That is one of the things that troubles me. Freda deserves more than I can offer her. Sometimes I wonder if I should not free her to marry someone who lives in Salem, or Pleasant Plain, or even Iowa City!"

"Jacob," I said with conviction, "I know Freda loves thee as much as thee loves her. That kind of love only comes once—or twice, at the most—in a lifetime. Thee must hold on to this woman, no matter what the cost. And that is where my idea comes in!"

"What idea?" he asked warily.

"Well, thee knows this cabin is much closer to Salem than the cabin thee, Mother and Father, and Levi live in. It would make a great deal of sense for me to move back home and for thee and Freda to live here."

"I would not think of having thee move from this cabin! This is the home Joshua built for thee, and thee should stay here!"

"Even though Joshua built the house, without his presence it is just another cabin. No one comes to me for treatment now, and in all honesty, I am lonely here."

"I am sorry, Rebecca. I wish I had more time to spend with thee."

I laughed aloud, probably the first good laugh I had had since Joshua died. "Jacob, thee has been the only one who *has* visited me—at least the only one I have felt at ease with. Without thee, the days would have been unbearable!

"Thee does not have to give me an answer today; go home and talk about it with the family, and by all means discuss it with Freda. It seems to me, however, that it might be the best thing for both of us!"

Eventually, Jacob and Freda did decide to move into our cabin when they were married. Freda seemed to want to make some changes, yet I knew she was reluctant to do anything for my sake.

"Freda," I told her as gently as possible, "thee does not need to worry about my feelings. I have dealt with death and loneliness and thee can be certain that a few changes in this cabin will not affect me!"

I did not move back to the family cabin, however. Even with the additional room that would be mine, I felt the need to continue to be on my own—free to come and go when I was needed. Of course, I was still barely able to keep busy, as no one was seeking my services.

My decision in the end was to rent a room in Salem for the time being. Jacob would continue to farm my land, and we would share the proceeds. I hoped that between the farm income and patients I would be treating there would be enough money to live on. My needs were simple, and the rent was not great.

I did not tell Charles I was moving, so when he saw me

leaving my rooming house one morning early in the tenth month, the perplexed look on his face made me smile.

"Rebecca," he shouted, pulling his buggy to the edge of the street where I was walking.

"What are you doing...I mean, why did you come from the rooming house...oh, please forgive my curiosity. I have been so negligent where you are concerned! I have no right to ask you anything!"

"That is all right," I said, a smile of pleasure crossing my face. I noticed some changes in him—his coal-black hair was beginning to get a few streaks of gray, and a slight bulge could be seen where formerly a flat stomach had been. But his eyes were still as bright blue as ever, and he looked wonderful to me at that moment.

"Is there something wrong, Rebecca? Did I spill breakfast on my shoes, or do I have food on my face?!" he said, noticing the way I was staring at him.

"Now it is I who must apologize. It really is good to see thee again, Charles. I have missed our visits," I said simply.

"Would you have time to go with me to visit a couple of patients? I was just on my way to the Simmons' farm when I saw you."

"Well..." I hesitated, not really knowing if it would be proper for me to be seen riding with Charles. Even though Joshua had been gone for seventeen months now, I did not want any suspicions raised.

"Rebecca," Charles said gently, "you and I worked together in the past, and we can begin to work together again. I have been so busy these past few months it would be a relief to have some assistance. Surely no one would question the relationship of a doctor and his assistant!"

"First of all, I did not move to Salem to become thy assistant," I said firmly, wanting to set the record straight right from the start. "I moved here because Jacob and Freda needed a place to live once they were married."

"I know that, Rebecca. But surely you do not want to

abandon your practice just because you have moved to Salem!"

"What practice?!" I asked bitterly. "I have no practice. It is as if people are afraid of me! No one comes for me, and no one asks for my help!" I finished, not realizing just how much it had affected me.

"Please, Rebecca, go with me on my calls so we can continue our discussion. There is so much we need to talk about."

Reluctantly, I took Charles' extended hand and climbed into the buggy. Surely I would not see many friends here that I knew.

"I'm sorry about your situation. I had a feeling that was happening, due to the increase in business I have had lately. I think it is just a matter of time, Rebecca. Folks around here believe you are still in mourning for Joshua, and they are reluctant to ask you to come to their aid."

"But do they not know that being active is exactly what I need to help me get past the mourning and on with my life?" I asked angrily.

"No, I am afraid they don't. There are some women who grieve for years over the man they loved. Most of them are not as strong as you are, however," he said admiringly. "As I said, I am certain that in time they will see you are doing well and again seek your services—especially now that you are in Salem. There are many times I am out of the office when an emergency arises. I have no doubt that eventually you will be as busy as I am! Of course," he said slyly, adjusting his position to look at me, "if you were to begin working with me in the office on a regular basis, everyone would know of your desire to see patients again!"

"Thee is a wily fox, Charles Jones!" I said with a laugh. "Thee could charm a cobra!"

"That is the first time anyone has called me charming!" he said, his eyes twinkling.

Suddenly, the oppression of the past several months began to lift, and I knew I would accept his offer to work with him once again.

"When would thee like me to begin?" I asked, suddenly feeling shy around this man I had at one time felt very close to.

"Today, of course! I missed Freda's help more than I could have imagined when she was away at school. I am hopeful she will return to her work in the office once she and Jacob are settled into their married lives."

"I suppose when that happens thee will not need me," I said stiffly.

"I could use three or four assistants if I could get them! What would work best would be for Freda to assume care for the people living around her home, and that you and I could care for the needs of those here in Salem and to the east. How does that sound to you?"

"It sounds like a good plan, but I am still concerned that people will think I am immoral for working with a widower so soon after my husband's death!"

"Well, let's think about it for a minute. You would be helping to save the lives of those around you...correct?"

"Yes...."

"And if you do not work with me, you will sit in the rooming house day after day until your mind ferments and your body grows stiff!"

"What a lovely picture you paint!" I chided him.

"I am quite serious, Rebecca. It will do you no good mentally or physically to be inactive. And as far as I am concerned, not using your God-given abilities to be of service to those around you is...is...a sin!" he blurted out.

"Well, thee certainly knows how to pull out all the stops," I said with a grin. "When you put it that way, I suppose I have no choice!"

"That's wonderful!" he said, a huge grin breaking his somber features. "I dreamed that some day this might happen, but I had no idea it might be so soon!"

"So thee had this planned all along, did thee not?" I asked, trying to gently put him on the spot.

"Why wouldn't I want to once again work with the best assistant I've ever had! You understand my needs as a doctor before I ask, and your knowledge of medicine is far beyond that of the average lay person."

"Keep talking, doctor! Thee is flattering me, I think, but it certainly sounds good."

"I'm not flattering you! Seriously, you are the best, Rebecca. I would not have said it if it were not true."

"I thank thee. But then, it seems I am always thanking thee!"

"I should be the one doing the thanking. You have always believed in me, and that has made these past few years some of the most pleasant since I was first married!"

Sensing the conversation to be going somewhere I did not want it to go, I quickly began asking about the patients he was currently treating.

The time spent with Charles went by so quickly that before I knew it he was escorting me back to the rooming house.

"So... will I see you tomorrow?" he asked, leaving me at the door.

"Bright and early," I said cheerfully, gently closing the heavy door behind me.

Having made the decision, I felt suddenly free. It was right for me to help those in need, and if it meant working with Charles, I would do it. As for developing anything else with him, I would simply work hard to maintain my distance. Even though Joshua had suggested I might build a new life with this man, I was determined to remain a widow the rest of my life.

I had learned to love and care for a man once, but it was simply too painful to lose him. I would avoid future involvements with any man. Period.

Fortunately, a member of the Society of Friends was not to remarry for at least a year, and most thought one should remain alone much longer. I had no desire to be separated from my many Friends by engaging in questionable behavior.

I would throw myself into my work and carefully guard my emotions. I, Rebecca Frazier, was a woman of the fifties. Single, independent, and a service to society. Once again my life was settling into a comfortable pattern, for which I thanked God that night and every night thereafter!

20

Blessings

My work with Charles was truly a blessing from God. Not only did it keep my mind occupied, it also filled the days and sometimes nights with opportunities to serve others.

Charles was patient with me, almost to the point of patronizing! "Charles," I finally said one day after he had asked me three times if I needed to rest, "I am not an invalid! My body has always been durable, and my emotions are stronger than ever. Thee treats me as though I were a fragile piece of china!"

After that statement, he seemed to relax and offered his apology. "I am truly sorry, Rebecca. Everything you have just said is true, I'm afraid. I just didn't want to push you too hard. It is so wonderful to have you working by my side once again. I didn't want to take any chances on losing you!"

"Does thee have any idea how much these past few months have meant to me?" I asked. "Thee has helped my spirit heal. The loss of Joshua was greater than I could ever have imagined. When I also lost the work I loved, my life nearly came to a standstill.

"Does thee believe in coincidences, Charles?"

"As a matter of fact, I have always believed that the timing of events is controlled by God, though sometimes our human intervention interferes with his perfect timetable. Why do you ask?"

"Remember the day I walked out of the rooming house just as thee drove by?"

"How could I forget?! That was the luckiest day of my life!"

"There thee goes, claiming God's timing to be luck!" I laughed. "I believe God sent both of us on our destinations at exactly the same minute in order for his plan for me—to work again with thee—to be set into motion."

"What makes you think I didn't just happen to know when you might be coming out and intentionally drive by at that time?"

"It might interest thee to know, Charles Jones, that I had been purposely avoiding thee for over a month. Thee did not even know I was living in Salem until thee saw me that day."

"It might interest you to know, Rebecca Frazier, that I had known for several weeks that you were living just down the street from my office!"

"If thee had known that, why did thee not seek me out to try and convince me to return to work?" I asked, his news a bit disconcerting.

"I was hoping that I would cross paths with you some day—just as we did—and that way I could speak with you casually rather than formally asking for your assistance."

"But when we met that day, thee seemed surprised to see me. Was that just an act? Had thee been spying on me all along, waiting like a cat ready to pounce at the first sighting?" I was not comfortable with these new revelations. I had no idea Charles could be that manipulative.

"I love the fire in your eyes when you get angry!" he said with pleasure. "And no, I did not wait to pounce on you, as you so gracefully put it! If you will recall, I was busy day and night with my practice. I hardly had time to plot a secret rendezvous! One of my friends at meeting said he thought Jacob and Freda had moved into your old cabin, and that you might be here in Salem since he knew you were not living with your parents.

"Now...how many places are there to stay in this one-horse town?"

"I might have been staying with friends," I said pointedly.

"Yes, but I knew most of your acquaintances, and I managed to work your name into several conversations to see if anyone might confess to knowing where you were living."

"Oh you did, did you?"

"Yes, and I am not ashamed to admit it. Rebecca, I have cared about you—more than you realized, I'm sure—from those first few weeks we worked together. When you were grieving for Joshua, I thought it best that I keep my distance. I did not forget about you for a day, though. Yes, I had my 'spies' if you will, but it was only because I cared deeply for you and I wanted to make sure you were all right."

"You could have come to visit me more than once," I said, disturbed by the implication of his words.

"I wanted to, Rebecca. You'll never know how many times I prayed to God, asking Him for the freedom to go to you at the cabin. But I never felt the confirmation of the Light, and I knew to make a call would only have been for selfish reasons. Do you understand what I am saying?"

"Yes, I suppose, but I would have thought an occasional visit for encouragement would have been acceptable," I said, rising from the paper work I had been doing to prepare to leave. I needed to get out of the room before Charles said something I did not want to hear.

"Then let me make my reasons crystal clear," he said with conviction, moving from the instruments he had been cleaning to block my path. "I did not come to see you after that one time because I could not trust myself. I love you, Rebecca. And once I was honest with myself, I realized I had loved you for a long time—probably since the day I shared with you about Julia and our baby. You helped me heal from the loss, just as I want to help you completely heal from yours." He now stood within a foot of me, and I knew he wanted my response. But my tongue was frozen, and I bit my lip to keep the tears from spilling.

Somehow, deep inside, I had always known Charles felt that way about me. But my allegiance was to Joshua, and always would be.

"I am sorry," I whispered as I grabbed my coat and fled out the door.

I spent the rest of the day walking, thinking, and praying. Though it was the first of the twelfth month, the air was mild and the walk seemed to clear my mind. I would have to tell Charles I did not care for him in the same way he did me. Even though it might mean an end to our working together, I was hopeful we could resume our former relationship.

As it turned out, Charles was the apologetic one. When I returned to the office the next day, he asked my forgiveness for saying what he had said, and assured me the subject would never come up again unless it came from me. I thanked him, and once again we became best friends.

The next few months were some of the most enjoyable of my life. Charles and I spent most of our days together, and I found his sense of humor to be one of his best features. Many times I would find myself laughing until my sides hurt at the stories Charles would tell of some of his first patients.

I had also begun attending Salem Friends for worship. Although I still felt strong ties to East Grove, it was nearly impossible to travel during the snow of the winter months, and once I began to know the Friends in Salem, I continued to worship there. When Charles offered to stop for me one Sunday, it quickly became a ritual, one we both seemed to enjoy.

If it had not been for Jacob and Freda, I would have transferred my membership from East Grove. I knew, however, the meeting was struggling to hold its members, and I wanted them to know they had my support. I continued to make contributions on a regular basis, as well as offering my prayer support.

In the fourth month I was surprised by a visit from Abigail and her new baby. After losing her firstborn, she was beaming with joy as she let me hold Mary Martha.

"I am so glad Daniel brought thee for a visit," I said after we had discussed the baby at length. "I just wish he could have stayed and visited for a few days. I know Jacob and Freda would have loved to have had a chance to see him."

"I tried, Rebecca, I really did. But Daniel was adamant about not being gone for more than a day or two at the most. The Railroad is busier than ever, and he is so afraid he might miss helping someone. It is admirable, but at times I get a bit disturbed with the way it consumes his every thought!"

Her words brought back memories of my own impatience with Joshua. Perhaps I could help my sister avoid some of the mistakes I had made.

"I know it must seem as if he cares for his passengers more than he does for thee and Mary," I began. "In fact, I felt the same way about Joshua and his need to always be off helping some other member of meeting with their problems. It took me a long time to realize that this compassion he had for others was what made him the special person he was! And it was not until I became aware of his illness that I realized just how much I loved him!"

"I know thee is right, Rebecca, but it is hard sometimes. I love Daniel with all my heart, and perhaps I need to let him be who he is rather than trying to change him."

A wistful smile crossed my face. "Thee has just found the key to happiness!"

"Now, what about thee? I know thee is still working with Dr. Jones. Does thee think...I mean, is there any chance...oh, never mind. I should not be asking thee personal questions on our first visit since Jacob's wedding!"

"It is all right, little sister! What thee wants to know is if there is a future for Charles and me. And the answer is yes, but only as a doctor and assistant."

"Oh, I am sorry to hear that. It has always been evident to me that this man holds a special place in your heart. I have seen the way thee looks at him, and thee always speaks so warmly about his work. I had hoped he might some day feel the same about thee."

"As I said, Joshua was my love, and I feel a need to remain true to that special love he had for me."

"I may be the younger sister here, but I think thee is foolish to hold on to the past when there might be a bright future ahead. It will be two years next month since Joshua passed on. I cannot imagine he would want thee to carry a torch for him even this long!"

Again Joshua's final words to me echoed that truth. He had wanted me to seek a relationship with Charles.

"No," I said slowly, "Joshua did not want me to remain alone. In fact, he even suggested I might find happiness with Charles."

"Then how can we help thy doctor friend see how much he could gain by falling in love with the best assistant in town?"

I felt a warmth spread on my cheeks as I finally admitted the truth. "Charles has already declared his love, Abigail. I was the one who turned away."

"But why, Rebecca? Is he not everything thee would want in a man?"

Finally, I knew I had to share the truth. "Yes, he is everything I could ever want in a man—and more. But that is the problem. If I let myself, I could love this man in a way I have never loved anyone before. It would not be fair to Joshua, when he loved me in that special way."

"Rebecca, this is nonsense. Joshua is in heaven, rejoicing with the Lord. He would want this for thee. Thee must forgive thyself for not being able to love him in whatever way thee thinks thee came up short, and allow God to give thee the desire of thy heart!

"Has thee been praying about the matter?" she asked.

"No," I admitted, "I suppose I thought I knew what God wanted me to do."

"But that is the problem! Thee is trying to intelligently analyze a matter of the heart! I am certain that if thee will pray specifically about a future with this man, the Light within will reveal the truth. And when that happens, there will be another marriage in the family!"

"I will take thy advice, Abigail, and pray about it. But do not expect wedding bells in the near future!"

I then quickly changed the subject, asking about common friends and the Springdale Meeting. We talked about Daniel's cousin George who had indeed joined John Brown's "army" when Brown had come to train at Springdale. Sadly, she told of his death with Brown and the other followers at Harper's Ferry when they tried to forcefully end slavery.

Daniel had felt badly for his cousin, but he had tried his best to dissuade him—to no avail. Daniel was more convinced than ever that war between the slave owners and those who opposed slavery was inevitable.

Our visit was over much too quickly, and I promised to keep in touch with regard to Charles. I also began praying over the matter, although I still felt no clear leading.

The summer months were pleasant, milder than normal with cool evenings. Charles and I had taken to walking when time allowed, sometimes driving to the country before beginning our stroll. It was on one such evening that my life was to be blessed once again.

As we sauntered along the river bank, Charles suggested we go for a swim.

"We did not bring extra clothing," I said, not really wanting to be soaking wet on the ride back.

"Then we could just go wading along the edge," he suggested.

The idea was appealing to me, and we quickly stripped to bare feet before beginning our trek along the shore. There had not been much rain lately, and the low river left a sandy ribbon that was just perfect for walking.

I was startled when Charles reached over and clasped my hand in his, but I did not protest. It felt strong and warm. Just like the man it was a part of. We spoke of trivial matters, but it was as if we were sharing as one body. And suddenly I knew that I wanted to spend the rest of my life with this man, and know him in more intimate ways than as his assistant. I wanted to hold him, and kiss him, share all of life together. Maybe even...dare I think it? Have a child together.

"Charles," I said, suddenly aware of how deep my feelings ran.

"Yes, Rebecca?"

"Does thee think thee would be interested in starting a new life?"

"What do you mean? Move to another town? Start a new practice?"

"No, I mean does thee think thee would like to begin a new life with me? As thy wife?"

Charles stopped so suddenly I nearly fell. "Are you saying...do you mean...that you might love me after all?"

At those words I laughed aloud, the tension of so many months snapping like a taut string. "Oh Charles, I have loved thee for nearly as long as thee has loved me. I was just afraid to allow myself to express those feelings.

"It was my sister who persuaded me to give the matter over to prayer, which I have been doing. Then today, as we walked, the Light within seemed to confirm everything I have been feeling but denying for so long. I love thee, Dr. Charles Jones, and I would like to spend the rest of my life with thee—nights as well as days!"

Perhaps I was being a bit bold, but I had waited all thirty-two years of my life to experience the kind of love I was feeling at this moment. I knew it was God's will for me, and

I could not wait to tell the world.

The kiss Charles gave me spoke of the passion and love he held for me. Later we would laugh at the sight we must have made—two adults kissing in the middle of the river. But I hoped the feelings of that afternoon would never end.

Charles had given me renewed life, and I vowed to make this partnership last forever. Free at last to love unconditionally, I began to splash water at Charles, eventually soaking us both as we laughed, and played, and planned our new life together.

EPILOGUE

Charles and Rebecca became one in body and soul within a month of their river walk. The Salem Friends Meeting House was filled to overflowing as their many friends and patients came to share in their union.

They continued to practice medicine together, though Rebecca's time was greatly reduced after the birth of their first child a year following their marriage.

Though they would never forget their first marriage partners, they vowed to give the gift of themselves to each other, living their lives in service to the Lord.